VAMPIRE'S INDULGENCE

GENTLEMAN'S BOUNTY: BOOK TWO

DRAKE LAMARQUE

GREY KELPIE STUDIO

ISBN kindle edition 978-0-473-53741-8

Paperback 978-0-473-53740-1

Cover by a brilliantly handsome prince

Printed in United States of America via Kindle Direct Publishing

Published by Grey Kelpie Studio

2020 has been a rough year for absolutely everyone. I hope that this book gives you some much-needed escapism even if for a few minutes.

I dedicate this book to everyone who has done something kind in the midst of the global pandemic and to everyone who has lost someone. Stay safe, loves. Be kind.

CHAPTER 1

IN WHICH A STRANGE OBJECT IS DEALT WITH

J'd brought something back with me from a dream. I'd woken up from another Cult-inspired nightmare and there was something in my hand. Something I'd never seen before in the real world. A wooden figure, about as long as my palm, it looked like a witch's charm or a religious idol of some sort.

I waited on the bed, turning the strange wooden thing over and over in my hands and trying not to scream.

In my dream, the one I had *just* woken up from. the hooded cultist had called me 'chosen one' and handed me this. They'd said that it would take away the pain, but when I'd taken it from them it had made my tattoo twist horribly, which was the worst pain I'd ever felt.

Well, the pain in my back was the worst, but it had faded when I'd woken up. The pain from when the cult of the Unknowable Way had tried to... awaken it, or use it, or whatever it was they'd tried to do with it back when they kidnapped me in Casablanca.

I shuddered.

The less I remembered about *that night* the happier I was.

I was torn on how I felt about the little wooden figure. It had a head, two legs and little arms carved into its sides, and on its back?

It had the same tattoo as me.

Some part of me was drawn to it, wanted to hold onto it, make sure nothing happened to it lest the same thing happened to me in real life. Sympathetic magic was A Thing, I was pretty sure.

But most of me wanted to toss it into the sea and never look at it again.

Gabriel came in at a light jog, Dante immediately behind him.

"What is it now?" He asked, his tone as well as his choice of words putting my back up a bit. It's not like I *asked* to be at the centre of some magical eldritch death cult.

I'd just wanted to have a fun night, it wasn't my fault the magical eldritch death cult had chosen me to be the weird tattoo having tool to summon a horror from beyond the stars.

"Sorry to bother you," I said, acidly, which felt good. It felt better to be annoyed and pettish than it did to be afraid and confused. "Just another nightmare. This time I brought something back with me, I'm sure it's nothing much to *bother* you with."

Gabriel sighed. He pushed a hand through his beautifully golden hair, letting it catch the light just to spite me I'm sure, crossed the cabin and sat on the bed beside me. His bed. His shirt was half unlaced, because although it's generally agreed that I'm the whore on the Devil's Whore, Gabriel isn't so far behind in my opinion.

He was ridiculously handsome and attractive even when I was annoyed at him, of course.

Dante stood awkwardly next to the bed, folding his arms and then unfolding them.

"He did just have another nightmare, you might be a bit kinder," Dante muttered.

"I don't need your pity," I said, although truthfully I wanted pity from both of them. Truthfully, I wanted Gabriel to pull me into his strong arms, press me into his chest and tell me that he'd protect me from the world. And then he'd kiss me and we'd be naked together and...

No, I'm getting distracted again. Show him the thing.

I held the little wooden figure, warm from my hand, out to Gabriel on the palm of my hand.

"What is that?" He pulled a face as if it were a piece of decaying meat, or something a dog had left on the street. I fought the instinct to close my hand protectively over it.

"I don't know. I dreamed about it and then when I woke up it was there. I had it in my hand."

Gabriel sniffed and picked up the thing between his thumb and forefinger, looking it all over.

"Seen anything like this before?" He asked Dante, he tried to give it to him but Dante shook his head and kept his arms crossed. Gabriel placed it gingerly back in my outstretched palm and I gripped it instantly.

"Never," Dante said. "Although I've hardly dabbled in dream magic."

"Know anyone who does?" Gabriel asked.

Dante shook his head. "Vampiric magic tends to be ... well, a lot more blood based. I expect we could find a witch somewhere who'd know."

I reached my empty hand out to Dante and he finally uncrossed his arms and took my hand, squeezing it gently.

"Well, what should we do with it?" I asked.

"Toss it overboard? Burn it?" Gabriel suggested. "I don't like the thought of it being on the ship... watching."

"It doesn't have eyes," I said, before holding it up to check. No, the head was totally smooth.

"There's a chance it's linked to him," Dante said, moving closer to my side and bumping his hip against my shoulder. It was his way of being comforting when there was someone else in the room, I expect. Although Gabriel had seen us in a much more intimate clinch that this.

"That's what I was wondering," I said. "What if we threw it overboard and I started drowning? Well, I guess we could just try it out in a glass of water." Suddenly more curious than anything else, I turned to look for the jug of water Gabriel kept by the bed.

"No, Cedric," Dante said. His hand on my shoulder, quelling. Those two words together formed my least favourite sentence in all the world.

I sighed. "Well, what then?"

"I could lock it up with the ransom money," Gabriel tapped his finger on his lip. "Then at least no one else will get to it, and Cedric won't get himself into more trouble, experimenting on it."

"The lack of trust!" I exclaimed. Gabriel took the wooden doll from me, holding it a bit more confidently this time, and took it to the safe.

Dante gave me a concerned smile. "You're not feeling ill though, sunshine?"

I huffed a little but honestly, I was quite all right. Besides him using his pet name for me, which always gave me a little happy flutter, it was always nice when someone else solved one of my problems. Besides, I'd just remembered that Oliver had demanded I spend the night with him, which was a prospect sure to warm my soul. "I suppose not."

Dante leaned down and kissed the top of my head, which made me smile. I reached to pull him down by the back of the neck and kissed him on the mouth, feeling better and better. Perhaps locking the doll up was the best choice.

"Next time we make land you're taking that thing to a witch and we're getting some answers," Gabriel said. He'd closed the safe again and was now standing beside Dante. "And I don't like that you're still having the dreams. That cult leader's sister, I wish I'd killed her. She could be responsible for this." He sighed heavily. "We'd better get back before Marco sails the ship into a reef or something."

Gabriel ruffled my hair and I saw a flash of his smile, making my heart beat extra hard once or twice. "Please try and stay out of trouble for a couple of hours, puppy."

I stuck out my tongue playfully and promised nothing.

They might be ridiculously stoic and fearsome pirates to the rest of the world. But to me, they were just Dante and Gabriel, and they were sweet and affectionate and had given me adorable pet names.

CHAPTER 2

IN WHICH CEDRIC'S YEARS OF YEARNING ARE SOMEWHAT FULFILLED AND OLIVER LEARNS SOME MORE ABOUT THE SHIP

*O*ver dinner, sat at the table, I found myself watching Oliver, and thinking of his promise to me. That I would spend the night with him, and finally consummate the love I'd been nurturing for him for years. Could it only be two days since he'd visited me at my father's London house and I'd told him my feelings? It felt like a world away now.

Now, I was focused on his promise, and the intensely incendiary moment we'd shared earlier where he'd pounced on me and ground himself against me until I could barely breathe. My trousers got too tight just remembering, and thinking of how much better it would be once we were alone.

From the moment I'd first seen him, hired by my Father to be my tutor and chaperone, an unassuming young man with wire rimmed spectacles and sandy blond hair, I'd felt a flutter in my heart.

And tonight, tonight I would finally get to see him naked.

Oliver noticed me staring at him and outwardly didn't respond, but I felt a soft warm foot on my ankle, which brushed up my calf, and I felt a blush in my cheeks. Oliver smiled slyly and helped himself to another bread roll.

His foot ventured a little higher on my leg and I dropped my fork, sending it clattering against the plate and drawing everyone's attention to me.

"Just a little clumsy tonight," I said, picking it up again. "Nothing to worry about, gents."

Gabriel chuckled and Dante shook his head.

Oliver grinned at me and stood up and said. "Well, must be time to go to bed. Are you coming, Cedric?" He gave me a wink, and several of the crew laughed in a lewd manner, and usually I'd have laughed and made some crude joke to get them laughing even harder, but instead, an icy finger trailed down my spine and my mouth went dry.

I didn't know what was wrong with me.

Oliver wanted me to go to bed with him, right then.

And I'd been crushing hopelessly on Oliver since practically the first moment I met him. I stood up, and forced a laugh as Gabriel slapped my ass and told me to be good for Mister Stanhope.

Oliver held his hand out to me and I took it, with my heart in my mouth. The noise of the crew seemed to fade behind an ambient roaring in my ears.

"Are you quite all right?" Oliver asked, as we went below deck and he led me to his cabin.

"Mm? Me? Yes," I said. I swallowed and put on a bright smile. "Of course I am."

Inside the cabin it was very close. There was a bed along one wall, Oliver had a little desk and his luggage, and then there was him and me and the room seemed far too small for all the things in it. Oliver carefully removed his glasses and stowed them in the tiny drawer beside his bed.

"Because it sort of looks like you the blood has drained out of your face, and you're not breathing."

"No... blood?"

"You've gone pale." He let go of my hand and pressed his palm to my forehead. "And you feel sort of clammy."

What was going on? I was supposed to be devastatingly charming right now, seducing him with my wit. Instead, he thought I was sick.

Get it together, Cedric, you ridiculous arse.

"No, it's nothing, just..." I trailed off, trying to make sense of what I was feeling. Pressure? Dread? The fear of making a fool of myself when all I wanted was to impress him?

Oliver looked deep into my eyes and took a half step back. "Goodness, is it possible that you're actually nervous? I thought you'd done this dozens of times."

"I have, I... do." I rubbed my hand over my eyes and shook my head, realising the actual source of my sudden ineptitude. "But never..." I tried to swallow against the dryness in my throat and went ahead and told him the truth as I realised it. "But I've never done it with you."

It was utterly humiliating. But at least I'd been honest.

"That's very sweet," Oliver said. And from anyone else I'd have thought he was making fun of me, but looking into his eyes I could see he meant it, he was touched.

He took my hand and squeezed it gently. "I don't want to put any pressure on you, Lord knows I've waited long enough for this."

I tried to imagine Oliver waiting for me, but it didn't make a lot of sense. I'd always been the one pining for him. If only we hadn't wasted all that time in Kingston not kissing each other...

"I'm not meant to be sweet," I said, finally. "I'm meant to be seducing you with my urbane good looks and sophistication."

Oliver laughed, but in more of a friendly way than a mean way. "Cedric. I know you too well to be fooled by the moves you usually put on people you want to bed. How about you just be yourself?"

As if that's easy... I don't know the first thing about what he sees in me, and I don't want to mess anything up.

"Cedric. Stop thinking." Oliver leaned in and kissed me, and some of the tightness left my chest. This I knew how to do.

I kissed him back, pushed him gently towards the bed, following with my hands on his hips.

"I've wanted you for so long," I murmured, wanting to confess.

Oliver placed a series of sweet, tiny kisses up my jawline (I was glad I'd taken the time to shave before dinner) and I sighed, feeling the lump in my throat melt away.

His hands went to my shirt and started to unlace it in the front. I felt another shiver of ice and realised I wasn't done confessing.

"Wait, hold on, before you..." I took his wrist and swallowed. "Um, there's something else, in Casablanca... wait, the uh, the night before I was kidnapped in Kingston."

"Yes?" Oliver asked. He didn't stop undoing my shirt and now his fingers were on the skin of my chest. His touch was gentle but inflammatory, sending sparks of need through me and making my heart speed up.

"It was a cult," I blurted. Oliver's fingers stilled and he looked up at me.

"A what now?"

"A cult. They uh, they put a tattoo on my back, I've no idea how, and then they kidnapped me."

"I thought the pirates kidnapped you."

"They did. They did, and then the cult took me, and they tried to sacrifice me and there was some kind of crazy magic..." I shook my head. This wasn't exactly seduction material. But he had to know before he saw my back. "The thing is, they're still after me and that's why I didn't want to stay too long in London. I have no idea how many people are involved in the cult and to what lengths they'll go, so I have absolutely put you in danger by inviting you on the ship, and I'm sorry for it."

Oliver frowned and then nodded. "I'm so sorry." He slipped his arms around my waist and pressed himself to me. It was marvellously comforting.

"Well, you know," I said, stroking a hand down his back. "It was terrifying and I nearly died and oh, I still have nightmares, too."

He kissed the corner of my mouth and smiled. "No need to lay it on that thick, I already feel protective of you getting hurt. Now, turn around and show me this tattoo."

I should have known he'd see through my trying to milk the situation. I turned, he left his hands on my waist, and shrugged off my shirt, letting it fall to the ground.

"Hmmm." Oliver's fingers left my waist and traced the shapes that I was becoming unpleasantly familiar with. "That's... rather terrifying an image, isn't it?"

I bit my lip. "If you'd rather not... with me... after seeing it, I'll understand."

"Don't be a goose. It's not going to stop me wanting you." He pulled me backwards against his chest and kissed my neck. I hummed with happiness, inhaling the scent of him and placing my hand over his where it pressed on my stomach.

"I promise nothing."

I shivered, enjoying the feel of his body against mine and the scent of him, so familiar, and yet I'd never been *this* close to him.

I threaded my fingers through his and felt my panic ease off. I could do this, I knew how to do this, and just because it was with Oliver, who I'd loved for... I tensed again.

"Just breathe," he murmured. I'd never heard sexier words.

I breathed out heavily and pressed back against him, circling my hips a little to tease against the hardness I felt from him.

"Mmm." He kissed his way down my neck, so gentle and sweet that I got goosebumps. People weren't usually tender with me, I didn't think it was something that I'd wanted, particularly, but now that it was happening I found I rather liked it.

He let go and moved back, I turned to watch him undoing his trousers, letting myself drink in the sight of him in a way I'd only ever done before in secret. He was more muscular than a regular college-educated tutor, on account of working on the docks while he was studying. I imagined him hauling heavy barrels and the like and felt myself get still harder.

I shoved my own trousers down my hips and stepped out of them, now that I'd relaxed I wanted to be getting on with it. When one had been thirsting for so long, and then was offered a drink, one didn't waste time taking a sip, after all.

With that in mind I sank to my knees and stroked my hands slowly up his thighs, making eye contact with him as I leaned in and licked the end of his lovely long cock.

His cheeks flushed a little and his hand found its way into my curls. "Ohhh, Cedric, you don't mess around do you?"

In response I licked my tongue slowly up the length of him, teasing him as best I knew how, teasing around his frenulum, which was a word I only knew because of Oliver and his biology lessons. Not that biology had ever gone quite like this, more's the pity.

I was rewarded by Oliver losing his words temporarily and making a kind of delightfully exasperated moan. So I did that more, rolling my tongue around the sensitive spot and teasing at his foreskin until his fingers tightened in my hair and he tugged me back.

"Come up here, I want to come inside you but not in your mouth."

"Well, if you're going to be *vulgar* about it..." I said, laughing at my own wit.

I got to my feet and he stopped any further witticisms with a luscious kiss that weakened my knees, sending me crashing against him. He lost his footing and we both landed on the bed in a tangle of limbs. I couldn't stop kissing him though, and used the opportunity to climb up him and tease at his cock with my ass.

Oliver's hand struck out to the side and he fumbled in his

bedside drawer, pulling out a very familiar looking pot of oil. I had hardly expected Gabriel and Oliver to shop at the same store for their sex supplies, but at least I could tell this one was sealed - Oliver hadn't borrowed it off Gabriel, which was something of a relief.

He seemed to be struggling with the wax seal one-handed so I took it off him and sat back a bit, putting more of my weight on where I was grinding against his cock. I stilled my movement and opened the pot of oil, moved up onto my hips and began to prepare myself with both hands.

Oliver groaned again, his hands stroking over my waist, my hips and up to my chest. His eyes were hooded, watching me. He'd have made a sinfully delicious portrait in the moment. I imagined rendering his likeness, from the chest up, and that expression... he'd have women tearing their bodices off and men reaching for the oil pot. Perhaps it was better that no one saw him like this but me.

I was torn, this moment was intoxicating, and part of me wanted to take my time, but a larger part of me wanted to get on with it, it felt as if I'd engaged in several years of foreplay with Oliver, and I wanted release.

I rolled my shoulders, trying to hold off on the impatience a little longer.

"Fucking hell, Cedric."

"You know, I think that's the first time I've heard you swear."

"Wasn't supposed to while your father was paying me," he gasped. "Supposed to set a good example."

"No one's paying you to be good now," I said, panting a little myself now from stretching myself open and watching him watch me like I was something he really, desperately wanted. I basked in the way it made me feel. Oliver, who I wanted so badly, wanted me in return. It was a heady, delicious feeling.

I positioned myself above him. "Ready?"

He sat up and pulled me to him, kissing me hard enough to

distract me. He rolled us over and I looked up at him in surprise. "Yes, are you ready?"

I almost said no, just because my heart was so full and I wanted him so much, but that was foolish. "Of course." I leaned my head up to kiss him again, just as he pushed inside me.

He felt perfect, there was just no other word for it. It wasn't like being reamed by Gabriel (which I loved) or the needy way Dante fucked me (which always included a deliriously good bite), he wasn't being gentle exactly, but he was gentle*r*.

"Enjoy this, Cedric," he said, cupping my cheek with one hand and smiling something rather wicked. "Because the next time we sleep together it's going to be a lot rougher for you."

"I-it is?" I hiked one leg up beside his hip, inviting him in deeper, and he took the invitation gladly, tipping his head back and groaning. A sweet, almost musical sound that I resolved to hear at least a thousand more times before I died.

"Next time, I'm going to put you over my knee and spank you like the bad boy you are," he said, his head still tilted back, exposing his graceful neck. I clenched around him involuntarily and my cock got harder still, throbbing where it was caught between our bellies.

"All that time and you were so adorable and so ... annoying. I couldn't get the idea out of my head," he said. Then he shook his head and made eye contact with me again. "But that's for later. For now you should tell me how much you want me."

My mouth had gone dry and the shock of what he had said scrambled me for a moment but I rallied admirably quickly.

"I want you so much," I said, and then felt it wasn't enough so I continued. "The colour of your hair in the sunlight is dazzlingly beautiful. I'm entirely enamoured of the shapes of your arms, those muscles." And then it occurred to me that I could be touching those very arms, so I did. I ran both hands up and down his arms, feeling the golden softness of his downy hairs, and the hard, shifting muscle beneath it. "Just gorgeous."

"That's it," he said. He sneaked a hand between the two of us and closed it around my cock, stroking me slowly, in time with the movement of his hips. I wrapped my legs around his hips and groaned, digging my fingernails into his bicep.

"I'd let you do anything to me," I said, which wasn't at all what I'd planned to say, but it seemed to be an unconscious response to his threat to spank me. "I love you, Oliver."

"I love you too, Cedric." He turned his head and kissed the back of my hand where I was scratching his arm and it was such a sweet, romantic gesture to do while he was inside me that I almost cried just from the sheer beauty of it all.

He kept eye contact with me as he thrust and stroked and I felt his arms and then his chest and groaned over the gorgeousness of him and how good it felt to actually be allowed to do this with him, and that he wanted to do it with me as well.

We came together without prompting, naturally moving in perfect time, revelling in each other's bodies.

Afterwards he cleaned me up gently with a damp cloth, pulled me into his arms and nuzzled his nose into my hair. "Tell me, Cedric, was it everything you dreamed it would be?"

I shuffled myself back against him, pressing my back harder against his front. "Better," I said. "But also I'm very much looking forward to the spanking. I will admit, I imagined it myself once or twice..."

Oliver laughed against my hair, and I started to doze off, feeling sure that with him protecting me from my cursed tattoo and from the universe, I should only have sweet dreams.

CHAPTER 3

IN WHICH MORE TRUTHS ARE TOLD

I was woken by the clanging of the alarm bell, and Oliver startling against me.

"Good God, what is that?"

"Don't say God," I mumbled. "Dante can't abide it..." But my own senses were on alert as well. "Maybe someone's attacking us?"

"Attacking us, oh God, pirates?"

"No, it's..." I sat up, my stomach sinking as I realised I needed to confess yet another thing. "No, the Devil's Whore is a pirate ship."

"I know the Devil's Whore is a pirate ship. Everyone knows that, it's the most feared ship on the seas, after the Grey Kelpie." I sat up and Oliver scrambled past me on the bed and pulled on his trousers. "We have to help defend-"

"No, this is - this ship is the Devil's Whore," I said. I reached for his arm. "You don't need to help, they're very efficient."

Oliver stopped when I touched him. He turned to me, his expression bewildered. "What are you telling me, exactly?"

"Captain Gabriel, well he's Gabriel on land when he needs to be a gentleman, and then on the seas he's Captain Lucifer. And this ship is the Whore."

"Didn't he kidnap you?"

"Yes, absolutely," I said, grinning. "It was hot as fuck. Hot as hell, even."

Oliver sat down on the ground and I'm not sure he'd entirely planned to do it. "Cedric. You chose to sail off with the pirates who kidnapped you?"

We could hear shouts and thumps from the deck above us. It did sound rather serious, but Gabriel hadn't stormed in to chain me to the bed so I expected it wasn't such a terrible attack. Well, the alarm had rung, so it wasn't nothing... but going up to the deck and getting in the way of the crew would be counterproductive and dangerous.

I reached to tug Oliver back to his feet and then onto the bed beside me, he let me do it but he didn't sit so close. He looked annoyed.

"Yes, well, they're good pirates," I said.

"Good pirates?" Oliver shook his head and sighed and I felt like he was about to tell me to go study my Latin so he didn't have to look at me any more.

But he couldn't do that, because he wasn't my tutor any more, and besides, we'd fucked and then slept together all night, limbs tangled together and his breath on my neck.

I squeezed his hand.

"I know what it sounds like, believe me, and I don't blame you for being annoyed. But the fact is, they are good pirates, and Dante's a good vampire, and besides all of that they protected me from the cult and they rescued me when the cult was going to... I don't know. Sacrifice me? Use me as a portal for a horrible monster who lives behind the stars?" I scrubbed my free hand through my hair. "I don't think I'm explaining this well at all. How about you ask me questions and I'll answer them."

Oliver took a deep breath and huffed it out. He lifted my hand and kissed the back of it, sighing heavily directly after, which rather undercut the sweetness of the gesture.

He dropped my hand and pinched the bridge of his nose, his eyes closing.

Aah, I've given him a headache. Yes, just like old times.

"Cedric, how do you manage all this? How do you constantly attract trouble? And keep on surviving against -" he was cut off by a booming noise and the ship canting to one side. The cannons had fired. Oliver's eyes cut to the door and then to the ceiling.

"It's fine," I said. "Go on."

"You keep surviving and anyone else would just... give up, or go into hiding or, I don't know. Run away from the world, but you just keep on going?"

I shrugged. "I don't know, it's exhausting to be sad all the time, I suppose."

Oliver blinked at me, his expression utterly blank.

"I mean, I do get sad. I wallowed for days when Gabriel said he'd give me away for the ransom money, but it all worked out all right in the end."

Oliver squared his shoulders and looked at me hard. "You're absolutely impossible."

"I'm aware," I said, allowing myself to smile and move a little closer to him, seductively. I was still naked, so I was hoping it'd have a nice effect on him. "But you love me, and you knew I was impossible even before you said that."

"I did..." Oliver's lips tugged into a slight smile that he tried to quell. "Cedric, the ship's under attack, I don't think this is really the time."

I leaned closer and ghosted my lips across his jawline, feeling the stubble and feeling tempted to just bite at him.

His hand found my shoulder and gently guided me back. "Wait, did you say *vampire?*"

"Oh, yes. He uh, well, he has a witch charm so he can out in the daylight, and he feeds off enemies, and off me. It actually feels really good. Like, well. I like a bit of spice, a bit of pain and it's like, the best of all of that." I sat back on my heels and looked at him hopefully. Maybe he'd take the hint and fuck me again.

"I wasn't aware vampires existed outside of stories," he said.

I shook my head. "Me neither! But I've seen it now, it's amazing what he can do. His fangs pop out and everything."

Oliver nodded slightly. "Fascinating," he said. And it was sort of in a scholarly scientist-who-just-discovered-a-new-species kind of way and my hopes of some more sexy times began to evaporate.

In a last ditch effort, I touched his chest and let my thumbs trail down to rub at his nipple. "We can still amuse ourselves for now," I ventured.

His hand came up and caught mine and he shook his head. "Not now, Cedric, I have too many things to think about. Vampires are real? This changes a lot."

I flopped back on the pillows and sighed. "Fine."

Oliver got up and went to his chest, pulled out a handbound paper journal and a fountain pen, sat at the tiny desk and started to scribble away.

I amused myself by watching him and remembering everything we'd done the night before.

Oliver was absolutely right, I was impossible - I hadn't considered how other people might have handled all the things that had happened to me, but well, what was the point of worrying about things that had already happened? I had been terrified when Elder Harrow and his followers in the Cult of the Unknowable Way had me, of course I had. And I hated the nightmares the cult had given me, and when I thought too long about what would happen if they should ever catch up with me again I felt shivery... but there was no point ruining a perfectly good day with 'what ifs'.

Here, in this moment, sitting and watching Oliver write whatever he was writing down, I'd rather just think about how much I liked him, and how satisfyingly stretched and used my asshole felt.

And tonight I got to have a proper reunion with Gabriel, and maybe I could convince Dante to join in, too. And *that* was worth thinking about as well...

And maybe in a few weeks, I could convince Oliver that he might want to join in with me and one of the others, and how steamy would *that* be?

No, I didn't like to linger on the things that had already happened or the bizarre circumstances I found myself in. I'd much rather imagine nice things that lay in my future.

"Stop touching yourself while you stare at me," Oliver said without looking up.

I glanced down at my hand and realised that yes, I had been lazily stroking myself. I sighed and let my hand drop to the side.

"You're absolutely no fun, you know that, Ollie?"

"Don't call me Ollie, and I am a constant delight."

"Maybe we could do an experiment on how good your focus is while you're receiving pleasure from my mouth?"

Oliver crumpled up a piece of paper and tossed it at my head in response.

CHAPTER 4

IN WHICH PLANS ARE MADE FOR THE NIGHT

a cry went up from the crew up on deck, and from the jubilant tone of it I assumed Gabriel and his crew had been victorious once again.

"You all right doing this?" I asked, getting up and pulling on my clothes from the day before.

"Hmm?" Oliver looked up, half turned in the seat to blink at me. I'd interrupted him while he worked and he looked a bit befuddled.

"Are you suitably distracted? I'm going to go and see what all that was about, and lavish attention on the wounded. Perhaps I can provide some succour..."

"Oh yes, quite, go ahead," Oliver said. He turned back to the notebook. "Have fun with the succour."

I rather thought he was being cheeky with that comment, so I went and kissed the top of his head and tickled him under his chin just to distract him again. "I'll see what's out for breakfast as well."

He chuckled and caught my hand, kissing the fingertips before letting me go.

I walked out, leaving him to it, and it was only as I started towards the upper deck that it occurred to me that the cheer I'd heard could have been from the attackers, and the people I cared about could have been killed or captured.

My heart thumped a little, and I made my way up the stairs slightly slower, and hung back, peeking around the corner at the main deck.

Marco was wiping off his knife on a bloody rag. Kaito was tipping some unfortunate soul off the side of the ship, and Bilal was visible on the ship now lashed to ours.

I relaxed, looking around for Gabriel. He was looting the body of a tall man with broad shoulders and a nasty scar across his face. I made my way over to him.

"What was all that about?" I asked, casually as if asking about the state of the ducks on the Avon river.

"Some mercenary," Gabriel said. "Probably after the price on my head."

My chest released some tension I wasn't aware I was holding. I frowned, glanced up at the enemy ship, which was sort of angry looking somehow, and then at the other men on the ship. I realised what I was looking for - robes or strange people with grasping fingers.

"So it wasn't the cult coming after me?"

"No, there was no mention of you or the blasted cultists." Gabriel stood up and dusted off his hands before giving me a wide smile. "Hard as it is to believe, not everything that happens is about you."

"I don't see any reason I should believe that," I teased. Then I let him pull me in for a kiss, because I was so glad he hadn't been hurt.

Gabriel kissed me with gusto, tipping me backwards a bit, his hand in the small of my back as sturdy as a tree trunk, bracing me up, and I felt my heart flutter, as if I was some maiden he'd just rescued. I didn't mind that one bit. His body was hot from the exertion and I could feel it even through our clothing.

He set me back upright and winked - promising something more later - and then called out to Bilal to report on what they'd found over there.

I made my way over to Dante, who was dabbing at the corner of his mouth with a handkerchief.

"Cedric, good work on staying out of the way through all that," he said, which was a somewhat insulting way to be greeted, but I was relatively sure it came from a place of affection.

"Yes, well, rather thought you all had it under control. Besides, Oliver didn't know you were pirates, so I had to explain all that to him."

Dante blinked at me, his face a picture of disbelief. "You let him join the ship without telling him we're pirates?"

I shuffled my feet and dropped my eyes down. "Well, I thought he wouldn't come along if he knew. And I didn't know if he was going to come at all, so I didn't want to tell him anything that might jeopardize my chances, slim as they were. And he never asked."

Dante tutted his tongue against his teeth and I looked up to see him shaking his head.

Everyone was shaking their heads at me, and I wasn't sure I liked it.

"Besides, you kidnapped me, I might remind you."

"Well," Dante had the good grace to look slightly ashamed. "That was a different situation."

"Hm." I folded my arms and eyed him, feeling confident in my upper hand.

"You knew we were pirates, when we kidnapped you. Or at least, right after the actual act of the kidnap."

"Oliver's fine, he just needs a little time to adjust. Besides, he's sturdy, resilient and all that. He's quite interested in learning more about what a vampire can do, as well by the way," I gave Dante a confident smile and he frowned a little more.

"I don't wish to be studied, Cedric."

I swallowed, because that was probably exactly what Oliver wanted to do, but well, I didn't want to annoy Dante any more than I already had. "I'm sure he'll just ask you a question or two, nothing much to it."

I slipped under his arm and smiled up at him. "Besides, don't you want to tell us both about the dashing things you did, and how you saved me from certain death?"

Dante chuckled, squeezed me against his side and kissed my cheek. "Not particularly, but I'm getting the idea you want to hear me weave such stories."

"Indeed, and then you could act them out as well, naked," I said, smiling and imagining it.

"You're ridiculous. What are your plans for tonight?"

"Gabriel," I said, promptly. "But I'd like it if you were there, too."

"I'll see what the captain says." Dante nipped me lightly on the neck, just a little tease, and let go of me. "Now make yourself useful and help with the transfer of goods from the other ship."

I groaned long sufferingly, as if he were asking a great task of me, and then went to do as he said. No one was going to take their pants off for me in the immediate future, it seemed, so I might as well be useful.

CHAPTER 5

IN WHICH CEDRIC IS PROPERLY
REACQUAINTED WITH HIS PIRATICAL LOVERS

The ship had been running on a minimal crew of strong looking mercenaries, barely ten of them, and all had died or surrendered to join Gabriel. I asked him if he wasn't worried about loyalty and possibly being betrayed but he assured me this was the kind of thing that happened a fair amount in piracy. That night we feasted on food filched from the enemy ship.

"Besides, they've seen us fight, they know what will happen if they betray us."

The ship was in decent shape, so Gabriel deployed a few men to sail it behind us, with the eye to selling it at the next port. We anchored for the night in the cove of a small uninhabited island.

The dinner was grand and accompanied by a barrel of wine that made everyone on board a little more mellow. The festivities involved singing and storytelling, and even Oliver came out of his shell a little more, laughing with Bilal and visibly relaxing.

Gabriel made eyes at me soon after the last of the food was finished.

I took Dante's hand and raised my eyebrows at Gabriel. His

face cracked into a wide and wicked smile as he stood up. "Well, men, it was a good day's work today. But now it's time for me to leave you to it. Enjoy yourselves!"

"And you enjoy Cedric," Marco laughed, and Gabriel echoed the laugh back at him.

I glanced at Oliver, but he was smiling indulgently. He waved me off, giving me... well, he didn't have to give me permission. I supposed he was giving me reassurance that he didn't mind.

I smiled at him, yanked Dante to his feet and the two of us followed Gabriel to his cabin. The crew whooped and shouted encouragement. I waved graciously as I could, but Dante sped up his pace, obviously not wishing to prolong our exit and the attention from the crew.

Gabriel led the way into his cabin and Dante tugged me in behind him. I turned at the door, gave those watching a wave and a grin and then closed the door.

"Happy with yourself, are you?" Dante growled a little.

"Very," I said. I leaned back against the door as if I were in no hurry at all. "I get to spend the night with the both of you, why wouldn't I be happy?"

Gabriel was removing his boots, sitting on the end of the bed. "Entirely too full of yourself," he grumbled. Then he looked up and I saw the spicy glint in his eye, he was amused, he was just pretending to be cranky with me.

"Well, I'm sure you could make me full of you instead," I said, pleased with my quick wits.

Dante rolled his eyes and folded his arms, standing awkwardly in the middle of the room, apparently uncertain. Gabriel didn't dignify my quip with a response either but he licked his lips and eyed me up and down.

"What, are you going to tell me you didn't miss me?" I asked, teasing the both of them. "Because I know it's not true, I can see you both devouring me with your eyes."

"Of course I missed you," Dante said. He dropped his hands

to his sides and looked longingly at me, and then at Gabriel, chewing on his lower lip.

What, is he waiting for Gabriel's permission?

Am I?

Oh fuck, perhaps I am. I pushed myself off the door and started to walk towards him.

Gabriel leaned back on his hands and looked between the two of us.

"Come on, then," he said, and grinned. His bright azure eyes twinkled in the lantern light and I felt a liquid heat melt through my chest and all the way down.

"Is that how you seduce ladies?" I asked, pausing to shrug off my shirt.

"No, I put a lot more effort in with ladies," Gabriel said. He lifted one finger to beckon to me and my feet moved quicker, because even though I was teasing him I had no desire to keep him waiting.

"Aren't I worth the effort?" I asked, smiling, as I reached to touch his gorgeous blond hair.

"That sounds like a trap of a question," Gabriel replied. He placed both hands on my hips, pulled me in between his legs and kissed my chest. "But yes, I rather think you're worth effort, pup."

Dante shed his clothes, moved to the bed and sat beside Gabriel, leaning in to kiss his shoulder.

Gabriel pulled my trousers open and shoved them down my hips, dipped his head and licked his way slowly up my cock.

"Ohhh for the love of..." I stopped before I took the Lord's name in vain. "Dante," I finished. Gabriel chuckled and swirled his tongue around the head of my cock. My knees threatened to buckle.

Dante winked at me, and moved up on his knees behind Gabriel pulling his shirt open and off then running his hands over his sides and down to his hips. Where he went to work on opening his trousers.

Fuck, it was good to see the two of them mostly naked, and touching each other. And touching me.

I groaned as Gabriel straightened up, wiping his mouth and leaning back against Dante's chest.

"Come on then, puppy, show us how much you missed us," he said.

I didn't need more prompting than that. I climbed into Gabriel's lap and ground down on him, leaning up to kiss Dante over his shoulder. Gabriel's arms went around my hips, steadying me as I lost myself in the cool loveliness of Dante's lips.

One of Dante's hands caressed my cheek, smooth and slightly chilly. He broke the kiss to murmur in Gabriel's ear. "May I feed, Captain?"

All sorts of tingles shot through me, hearing him asking for permission. It was all too hot.

I held my breath, hoping that he'd say yes, and it never even occurred to me that *I* could be the one to say yes. Not in this room. Gabriel was in charge of both of us, and that was more than fine with me.

"Yes, if Cedric wants it," he said, his voice a soft growl.

"Yes, please," I said kissing Dante's temple.

"But first, you need to get over there..." Gabriel lifted me and placed me to the side, so all three of us were lying on the bed. I had rather been enjoying rubbing my arse on his stiff cock but I expected he had some kind of even better idea so I didn't protest more than a wordless whine.

Gabriel took Dante by the hair and pulled him in for a kiss. I started to stroke myself watching them, my breath coming too fast to be quiet about it, although I had no desire to come this way, I couldn't simply watch.

Dante groaned, his nails clawing at Gabriel's chest, until

Gabriel broke the kiss and pulled his head down, guiding his mouth onto Gabriel's hardness.

Then Gabriel leaned down, one hand curled around my waist to pull my hips in again, and he resumed his earlier job, licking at my cock, which was now leaking. My eyes rolled back in my head for a moment, then Gabriel pulled off again.

"No slacking on the job, pup."

I looked down at him, bewildered. He nodded significantly at Dante, and then I got it.

Keeping my hips where they were, encircled by one of Gabriel's warm, muscular arms, I leaned to the side, braced my own arm alongside Dante's thigh and took him in my mouth.

It was a deliciously difficult challenge to give Dante the best I knew I could do when Gabriel's mouth was working me over. I moaned as much as I licked, but from the noises Dante was making, he wasn't complaining either.

I wished, as I let my eyes rake over Dante's midriff and over to his jaw, working as he took Gabriel down his throat, that I could somehow watch this as it happened. Perhaps a judicious application of mirrors to the interior of the cabin, or perhaps I could try and render it in paint...

This idle dream was short lived, as soon I felt the heat pooling and the tightening of my balls that heralded completion. I applied myself more meticulously to swallowing as much of Dante's cock as I could manage. I choked on the length of it briefly, felt tears spring to my eyes, pulled off to take a breath and then did the same thing again.

Dante's hips bucked and he came, filling my throat with his seed, this spurred me into action as well, and Gabriel swallowed around me, and then licked me clean.

I pulled back to do the same for Dante, cutting my misty eyes over to watch as Dante kissed the tip of Gabriel's dripping cock. It was still hard, he hadn't come yet. Gabriel's hand was in Dante's hair, pulling him back.

"Fuck," I croaked.

"Mmm, indeed," Gabriel said. "I'll fuck you while Dante feeds, how about that?"

My elbows weren't too sure about holding me up, but every part of me wanted what he'd suggested. "Oh, yes please, Captain." I pushed myself up onto all fours and lowered myself down again onto Dante's chest, leaving my arse up for Gabriel to use.

I'm the luckiest boy in the entire universe.

Gabriel wasted no time in oiling his fingers and stretching me, which was rather the counterpoint to Dante's gentle kisses and soft caresses. He was stroking my hair, gently carding fingers through my curls and gazing at me with a soft smile that made my breath catch. I tilted my chin up, encouraging him to move down, and he obliged, feathering small kisses over my jaw and then my throat.

Gabriel pushed himself against me just as Dante gave me a playful nip, just a lovers bite, not a vampire's one. I gasped and concentrated on keeping steady so that Gabriel could push deep inside.

My eyes were closed now. One of my arms wrapped around Dante's shoulders and the other bracing me, planted onto the bed beside him. Gabriel put his arm around my middle and started to pound me. I gasped with the intensity of it, moaning out my desire, revelling in each sensation.

Dante didn't seem deterred by the movement created by Gabriel's fucking me. He licked my neck, teasing me, before sinking his fangs in and starting to drink.

Fuck, there's just nothing like this. Roundly filled and thrashed by a pirate captain and bitten by a vampire at the same time. Remember to breathe, Cedric, or you'll pass out from sheer bliss.

I hadn't thought I'd be able to, as it was so soon after the last round, but my cock had gotten hard again and was dripping. I managed to force out a hoarse "Gabriel, Captain, please!" Before I lapsed into moaning and heavy breathing.

Gabriel got the message though, and I felt his hand close around me, pumping me. It only took a few strokes and I was coming again.

The dark velvet pull of Dante's teeth in my neck heightened all of it, and I cried out loudly, my voice breaking as I felt Gabriel fill me as well.

Dante licked my neck again and I felt the warm tingle of healing. He took me in his arms as Gabriel withdrew, and held me as I tried to master my ragged breaths once more. I lay sprawled over him, legs tangled together.

Gabriel extinguished the lamps in the cabin and returned with a damp cloth to clean me up with. Then he lay beside Dante, and pulled the blankets over all three of us. Then he turned on his side and draped his arm over my back.

I was so perfectly, deliriously happy, that I might have whispered that I loved them. But I can't be sure, I think probably I just fell asleep.

CHAPTER 6

IN WHICH A DREAM IS ENDURED

*T*his time at least, I knew I was dreaming. I'd been in this situation enough times now... here I stood on the deck of the Devil's Whore, only it wasn't really the ship. It was the ship in my mind.

My feet were bare, and I felt a little cold. It was nighttime and the stars above felt oppressively close. As I gazed at them I realised I didn't recognise any constellations, the stars, when I searched them showed me no Orion, no Cetus, no recognisable planets.

What did that mean? Which stars was I looking at?

I swallowed, looking around. I could hear the repetitive wash of the waves against the hull of the ship, and the soft hum of the stars themselves.

Then there was another sound. The wet thump of something landing on the deck. Wet. Heavy.

Then a slow drag sound, and another thump. Were there multiple things behind me in this dream?

What could it possibly be? Some kind of large and angry octopus?

The merfolk, come to drag me under the water and drown me?

Some lost souls, drowned sailors, brought to the surface by the horrible powers of the cult of the Unknowable Way? To do what? Tear me to pieces? To hold me for the cult? To haul me bodily through my dreams and into their clutches? Is that how magic worked?

My mind's eye provided me with some awful images - rotten men with their eyes missing, green flesh tearing off their bones, reaching for me...

I strained to turn and look, I tried to force my eyes away from the stars but my eyes watered with the effort of it and for nothing, I couldn't persuade my head to drop or my body to turn. I was frozen in place.

I knew it was a dream, and that things in my dreams couldn't *really* hurt me, but still I felt the fear of whatever it was behind me.

Squelch.

It was getting closer. I felt sweat bead on my forehead and drip slowly down my temple.

It seemed to freeze as it trailed down my skin.

Sucking in a deep, ragged breath I forced my eyes to close. Perhaps without the stars in my eyes I would be free of their sway and could turn.

My limbs started to shake, I was shivering. There was a howling in my ears, either from a sudden wind or from the thing... things... behind me.

I let my breath out as slowly as I could, although it came out more like a hoarse groan.

Water swirled around my feet, icy cold, chilling me further. I bent, wrapping my arms around my waist. With an immense effort, I opened my eyes.

I was looking at my feet, which yes, were in several inches of brackish sea water. Little bits of seaweed and fine fragments of wood swirled in the icy water around my ankles.

Look behind you.

Turning wasn't happening. I braced one of my hands on my knee and tried to straighten up but it was hard, hard as getting out of bed when I had a very bad hangover.

There was another thud, accented with a splash, close enough behind me that I felt a little spray from the splash.

What is it? Look behind you.

My hand slid of its own accord up my leg and into my pocket, gripping the small wooden figurine in there.

Just turn your body and LOOK!

I woke up with a start, jolting and bashing my chin against Gabriel's shoulder, I must have been resting my head right beside where he lay on his back. He grumbled and started to sit up, one hand reaching for his sword.

"Ow..." I groaned.

Dante, who was right behind me, his arm over my waist, had startled as well.

His body pulled violently back from mine and when I turned to squint at him he was half up and crouching, his teeth bared like an angry gargoyle.

"And you both call me the dramatic one," I said, shaking my head and flopping back on the bed.

It wasn't yet fully light, judging from the light coming through the leadlight windows in Gabriel's cabin. But it wasn't fully dark, or I'd not have been able to see Dante so clearly.

Gabriel leaned out of bed and struck a match, lighting a lamp. "What happened?"

Dante sat back down, looking slightly abashed. "Cedric woke us. Was it another nightmare? I felt something negative in the room..."

I nodded. "Yes, the same cursed thing, only worse. There was something behind me, maybe many things, and the deck flooded." I reached for Gabriel to pull him back in, he settled sitting partially upright, propped on the pillows and I snuggled into his side, wanting his body heat.

His arm went around me and his hand gently stroked my back. Maybe if he kept doing that for a few hours my heart would stop racing.

Dante moved closer behind me but didn't touch. He possibly sensed that I wanted more heat than he could give me just then.

"This is fine, just, can you stop jabbing me in the side?" Gabriel muttered. I squirmed, pulling my right arm out from beneath me where it had been pressing against him.

My heart sank when I realised why he'd thought I was jabbing him. I pulled away from his grasp and sat up, slowly unclenching my fist to reveal the small wooden figure.

My stomach sank. This was certainly a bad sign, and it meant the thing itself had to be cursed, but I felt drawn to it somehow.

"I locked that in the safe," Gabriel said. He said it accusingly, as if I or Dante were somehow responsible. Well, I supposed I was responsible.

"I didn't break into the safe," I said, quickly.

"It's the magic... we can't stop it working just by locking the thing up," Dante said. "I imagine if you try and throw it away it'll find its way back into Cedric's hand again."

"What if we burned it?" I asked, feeling a creepy sensation in my stomach.

"It could be sympathetic magic," Dante said, shaking his head. "We can't risk you incinerating yourself."

"Not to mention the ship," Gabriel added. He sighed heavily, leaned over to look at the thing as I turned it over in my fingers, and got up out of bed. "Nothing for it, we need an expert. We'll change course and head for Tortuga."

He pulled his trousers on and crossed to his desk, pulled out a map and then stalked out to the deck.

I watched him go, Dante moved closer, leaned back on the

pillows and drew me onto his chest. He wasn't as warm as Gabriel when it came to actual temperature, but he could be warmer in other ways. I set the wooden figure aside and wrapped my arms around him, sighing.

"The Captain doesn't care much for magic," Dante said, softly. "He's not angry with you."

"I didn't think... well, maybe I thought he was a little annoyed with me." The light through the windows was getting lighter and Dante was lit by a soft grey glow that made him look softer than usual. "Will we find a... well, can a witch do something about the tattoo, do you think?"

Dante's chest rose and fell and I wondered, not for the first time, if he actually needed to breathe or he just did it for the look of the thing. "I don't know, Cedric. I hope so. At the very least we can get you something that will ward your dreams, like the charm you used to have."

I nodded and closed my eyes, although I knew I wouldn't sleep again.

"Thanks, Dante," I said.

"Of course, Sunshine."

CHAPTER 7

IN WHICH OLIVER DELIVERS ON PART OF HIS PROMISE

*W*e'd been sailing for Tortuga a week, and I'd been very much enjoying the increasingly warm temperatures, when Oliver cornered me in the hallway outside his room. I was walking from the galley back up to the deck, munching on a sweet roll when he got into my way.

"Hello, Oliver," I said. "Are you done with your morning watch then?"

"Yes," he said. I tried to step around him and he stepped into my way. "What are you doing?"

"Eating some bread," I said. "And ... being accosted by you, apparently."

"Too right." He grinned, and in the dim light his glasses hid his eyes. My heart sped up.

"I'm sorry, are you actually accosting me?"

His answer was to push me with both hands on my shoulders against the wall of the corridor. He moved close in, pinning me to the wall and kissing me forcefully. His tongue demanded entrance to my mouth and I willingly surrendered it.

I curled my hand around the back of his neck and moaned, bucking my hips against his to encourage him. I certainly hadn't expected this, but I welcomed it with every fibre of my being.

He broke the kiss, grabbed me by the wrist and hauled me into his cabin. "No need to be quite so rough," I said, through a smile, baiting him.

"I rather think there is," he murmured. He let go of my arm and closed the door behind him. I had barely time to open my mouth before he'd shoved me against the door, face forward this time. One of his hands was planted between my shoulderblades, trapping me there, and his other hand was working the fastenings of my trousers open and shoving them down.

"Might I ask..." I managed to say, in between gasps. "What exactly brought on this most welcome attack?"

"How polite of you to ask," Oliver said. He stepped away from me and I looked over my shoulder, watching him and leaning my shoulder against the door, as he set his glasses down and pulled out that most lovely little pot of oil.

He caught my eye. "That's not where I left you, Cedric."

I felt a thrill of excitement go through me, but unlike Gabriel, Oliver had established no rules about who was in command and what he expected me to do. And besides he'd promised a spanking. So I shrugged and took a deliberate step from the door.

"I suppose it's not," I said. "What are you going to do about that?"

He made a noise in his throat that I recognised from the days when he'd set me Greek to translate and I'd get bored after two words. It was irritated and indicated he was fast losing patience. And of course, he didn't have to have patience with me now.

He shoved me face first against the door again, banging my cheek against the rough wood. His hands were spreading my arse cheeks apart and daubing me with oil. I had barely caught my balance before he was shoving a finger inside me.

"Oh fuck," I gasped, my eyes closing as I adjusted to the feeling.

"Mind your language, Mister Hale-Harrington," he said,

effecting the dry tone he'd used while he was tutoring me. I shivered pleasantly and pushed my hips back, encouraging his finger deeper inside.

"What if I don't?" I groaned.

"If you don't, you'll be adding more spanks to the number I was already going to give you."

I squirmed as he withdrew his finger, rubbing myself against him wantonly. "You did promise…"

"Ah." He shoved me against the door again and nipped my earlobe before whispering. "But patience is a virtue, Cedric. And the more you think about the eventual spanking, the more you'll ache for it, and the more you ache for it, the more delicious it will be when I finally give it to you."

I closed my eyes and braced the palms of my hands on the doorway. "I had no idea you had such cruelty in you, Oliver. I thought you were such a *nice* boy." I was baiting him again. A sucker for whatever punishment he would choose to give me.

"No one is paying me to be patient with you." One of his hands dropped to fumble with his clothes.

"So, what are you going to be with me? Now that you're free to do what you like?"

"What do you think?" He growled and pushed his cock against my arse, slick with oil and demanding. His breath was hot on the back of my neck and I groaned, pressing back, urging him inside.

He shoved inside at my wordless urging and I bit hard on my lower lip. It had been some time since I'd been entered with so little preparation and it stung in the most delightful way.

Besides all of that I was absolutely revelling in the fact that Oliver had come to seek me out in such a way. He had been thinking of me, imagining doing this, and then he'd come to find me and do what he'd imagined.

I hadn't ever expected he would want me this much.

My heart was pounding with exhilaration but with the simple delight in feeling needed as well.

Oliver's hand wrapped around my left wrist and his other hand gripped my right shoulder, his nails digging into my skin even through my shirt.

His teeth found my earlobe again and he growled as he pounded me hard, burying himself deep with each thrust, hard enough to slam me against the door and I groaned loud enough for the whole ship to hear.

"Yes, fuck, do it!" I grated out between groans.

His hips slammed into me and in moments he was gasping, throbbing inside me. He let go of my shoulder and started pumping my cock instead. My moans got deeper still, needy and so full of desire I thought I might forget how to breathe around them.

"You want something, Ced?" He panted out. "You're going to have to ask for it."

At that point I'd have promised him the world, done anything he demanded. Asking for it was about the easiest possible thing to me in that moment.

"Please, Oliver, please let me come, please I need it so much."

"Come," he grunted in my ear. I felt him fill me at the same instant I lost control and came over his hand and, no doubt, the door of his cabin.

In a moment, he came to a stop, gently eased out of me and drew me against his chest, holding me close as we both fought to catch our breath.

"That was ..." I struggled to find the correct word to describe how exquisite the experience had been. But all I could manage was "Fucking brilliant."

Oliver chuckled as he tugged me over to the bed for more cuddles. "You really don't know when to mind your tongue, do you?"

I stuck it out at him playfully. "Well, it's a very talented tongue."

CHAPTER 8

IN WHICH OLIVER EXPERIENCES TORTUGA
FOR THE FIRST TIME

*T*he Devil's Whore pulled into dock at Tortuga three weeks later.

In this time, Oliver had largely adjusted to life on the ship. A few times he had Cedric to himself, and those times were very sweet in his memory. The two of them getting to know each other even better than before, without the barrier of Oliver having been hired to look out for him. It gave him a lot more licence to be himself, and not worry about some kind of poor performance review.

And it had allowed him to be as rough as he liked with Cedric, who seemed to absolutely love that kind of treatment, which was lucky. At various points in his life, Oliver had worried that his desire to be a little cruel or brutal to his lovers meant he was some sort of evil doer, or perhaps damaged in some way. But as it turned out, it just meant he was the perfect match for Cedric Hale-Harrington.

He reflected with some regret that he hadn't yet convinced Dante to allow him to study him, but he had noted a few observations all the same.

Captain Gabriel (or Lucifer depending on the day) was still something of a mystery. Although Oliver wished to know more of the man who shared Cedric's affections, he sensed that the man was giving him time to adjust. Perhaps he would get to know him on land.

He also wondered if any of the rest of the men aboard the ship had strange or wonderful stories to tell. He had been gradually building trust with them, helping out around the ship where he could. His experience on the docks had certainly come in handy, and he was quick to learn the workings of the ship as well. The crew were warming up to him, but he knew he had to continue to work on building trust with them all if he wished to hear all their stories.

He wasn't at all sure what to expect from Tortuga. Although the pirates told a lot of wild and bawdy tales of the port town, Oliver had no idea how much of what they told was true and what was an exaggeration. He assumed though that it was a place where he should mind his purse, and stick close to the crew for protection.

They moored in the mid-afternoon, both the Devil's Whore and the captured ship, which Kaito and Marco were in charge of and would sell as soon as possible.

Oliver was surprised to see the crew were all dressed up for the occasion. Captain Gabriel had put on an impressive outfit of entirely black clothes, and looked every bit the terrifying Captain Lucifer of which stories were told.

Dante had pulled his hair back in a sleek ponytail and wore a tailored charcoal grey waistcoat over a tidy white shirt.

Cedric, obviously, had needed very little prompting to dig out one of the bordering-on-gaudy waistcoat and jacket sets he had commissioned from the tailor he liked in Kingston. He was resplendent in emerald green and he was barely containing his excitement.

"Can you believe it, Oliver," he said, taking Oliver by the arm and grinning widely. "Tortuga! City of lights!"

"I rather think Paris has that name," Oliver said, drily, but he gave Cedric a smile all the same. It was almost impossible not to be pleased when Cedric was so generous with his own pleasure. His smile was infectious and his enthusiasm even more so.

"Well, Paris has nothing on this place, in my opinion."

"Also you can hardly call this a city," Oliver said. "It's a town at best, possibly just a village."

"Now Oliver, no one likes a pedant." Cedric barely waited for the gangplank to be secured before towing Oliver off the ship, leading the way as if he owned the place. Oliver hung back on his hand a little, slowing him until Gabriel could catch up.

Gabriel strode into the lead, his bootheels thudding on the marina and then making a pleasing ringing sound on the cobbles.

"We shall book rooms at the Pickled Oyster," Gabriel said, glancing briefly at Cedric.

"The Pickled Oyster! What a fantastic name," Cedric exclaimed. "I love it already."

Oliver was content to walk a step and a half behind Captain Gabriel, who, he felt, offered a certain amount of protection from the criminal element. He looked terribly impressive, tall with ice blue eyes and his black garb.

Oliver was very familiar with the docks of London, including the less savoury elements from his work there to pay off his university fees. But even so, the docks of Tortuga struck him as rough.

There were a lot of people eyeing Cedric up with hungry expressions, and it occurred to Oliver that any of them could be involved in the cult that was chasing him. He moved closer to Cedric's side, so Cedric was flanked between Oliver and Gabriel.

Dante stalked behind them, and a handful of the crew behind him.

The buildings were a little rundown, but there seemed to be stores, market stalls, more than a handful of pubs and plenty of people walking about, drunk and celebrating or starting fights.

Gabriel paid none of them any attention. He strode through the town and up to an inn with a painted sign reading "The Pickled Oyster".

There was a verandah out the front with a few wooden tables and chairs, a handful of people were drinking and eating at them. The double doors were open beside the verandah and Gabriel led the way inside. He went straight to the bar and negotiated with the buxom barmaid.

Dante leaned against the bar and kept an eye on the crowd. Cedric took Oliver's hand and squeezed it, and for a moment, Oliver wanted to snatch it back and try to maintain some decorum. But his eyes landed on a table where a red headed young gentleman was sitting in the lap of a huge bear of a man, who was nuzzling his neck, obscuring his face. Oliver squeezed Cedric's hand back and felt a bright flash of freedom, the likes of which he had never hoped to enjoy.

"Two rooms. One for me and Dante and one for you, young mister Stanhope. Marco's arranged rooms for the crew to use closer to the docks at the King's Folly."

He handed Oliver his own room key, which dangled from a piece of steel and had the number one engraved on it. "Thank you, please, just call me Oliver though."

"Of course, and Cedric can pick and choose where he sleeps, as per usual." Gabriel handed the other key to Kaito and pocketed the last one. "And in the meantime, let us get some..." he trailed off, his eyes over Oliver's shoulder.

Oliver glanced behind him, a thrill of fear speeding his heart up. Gabriel's eyes narrowed.

"Fucking Hell."

"What is it, Captain?" Cedric asked, looking in the same direction, his expression pleasantl confused.

Dante hissed his breath out and pushed off from the counter. He followed close behind as Gabriel strode towards the man with the redhead in his lap.

Oliver half pulled Cedric behind him on instinct, but Cedric immediately stepped past him and followed behind, no doubt hoping there'd be a fight. Oliver adjusted his glasses and followed as well, hand on the hilt of the pistol Dante had insisted he take from the ship's stores.

"Bloody Tate," Gabriel said, his voice cold and clear, ringing out over the general noise of the crowded pub.

"Is that? Did he just say Bloody Tate?" Cedric glanced over his shoulder at Oliver with an excited grin.

"This should be interesting," Dante said. "And not in the fun sort of way."

"Lucifer!" The huge man said, with a broad smile. "It's been a while."

"You owe me a galleon, an entire ship's hold of gold," Lucifer declared, his voice carrying easily over the silence. The tension in the room was palpable.

Tate's face fell and his eyes narrowed and he shifted the young man off his lap and onto the chair beside him, reaching for the hilt of his sword.

CHAPTER 9

*T*he voyage from Casablanca to Saint Vincent had been largely uneventful for Elder Natalia Harrow. Her quick exit from the family manor meant she hadn't had time to pack anything, and the pirates had burned the place down, further scuppering her plans to retrieve certain artefacts. However, she had managed to grab her late brother's book, and truly, that was the only thing that mattered.

It was a peculiar tome, and Rupert had never told her how he'd come to be in possession of it. He'd simply come back to their house in London with it one day and held it up for her to marvel at.

"Sister, I have found something truly remarkable," he had said, back on that dreary Winter's day. "Something that will make those little séances of yours look positively dull."

Natalia had scoffed and none too quietly. She had, after all, quite a reputation amongst the gentry for giving exceptionally good séances. She'd made contact with several spirits from beyond the veil and even on one memorable occasion summoned some sort of poltergeist. That one had required some tricky magic to dismiss again and had got her invited to some swanky parties from impressed attendees.

But Rupert had showed her the part of the book he'd translated from a strange and unearthly cypher and then she saw how right he had been. This book, which was enigmatically called "The book that cannot be known", had potent spells in it. Ones you didn't have to be a proper witch to perform, no, these spells were very easy for an ordinary person to master, you just had to be willing to spill a little blood.

And Natalia had never been the squeamish sort.

They had spent some months together, deciphering the meaning of the book - discovering the message behind it. That there was something greater than themselves. That they could be part of something so much more powerful, so beautiful and incredible that it would change the world itself.

Their research had revealed to them the Order of the Unknowable Way, named for the book. The Order had of course, been around for centuries, but it had been more or less dormant in the last hundred years, only a handful of devoted followers. Natalia and Rupert were enthusiastic new blood, and they immediately started to actively recruit.

And the idea had spread like wildfire. The rich and powerful loved a good secret society, and with Natalia's brilliant idea to host the Hellfire Club to recruit the right kind of people, well, it all escalated exceedingly fast.

Rupert and Natalia had worked hard to swell their ranks, to convince the members to be loyal and of course, to find a way to perform the ultimate ritual.

Natalia stroked her fingers over the spine of the book, opened it to the page with the ritual instructions on it. Heavily annotated in Rupert's spidery hand.

Once they'd chosen their target, the perfect vessel for the portal's power, the Chosen One, well, everything had fallen into place.

Minister Hale-Harrington had said such very rude things to Natalia, when she had extended an invitation to join the Order.

There had really been no need for him to speak to her in that manner.

Especially when the Harringtons and the Harrows had shared ancestry.

He should have welcomed her with open arms, should have taken up a robe, tithed his fortune. Instead... no. He'd told her that it was nonsense, and that no Hale-Harringtons would ever deign to join.

She told herself she didn't need to dwell on it, she had her revenge, even if it was proving a little slower than desired. Harrington's boy, Cedric, was in her sights. He had the tattoo, and as far as Natalia had read there was no way to remove it.

Of course, some of the book remained untranslated...

She turned to the page Rupert had been working on before the whole debacle in Casablanca. It seemed important. She found her fountain pen and continued his work, using the cypher key he had inscribed on a slip of paper and stored in the book.

The crew of the ship who had given her passage were more than happy to avoid her, and left her alone except to let her know when the meals were.

In three days she had the page translated and was ready to do the ritual. It invoked a being, some kind of helper or servant, who could assist with magic and the ultimate ritual. The page promised that this being, something or someone called Nyarlothotep, would grant vast powers to those in its favour. Natalia wondered if they hadn't done this ritual earlier, if the grand spell in Casablanca would have worked. Perhaps if she hadn't pushed Rupert to move as quickly as possible, he might still be alive.

She did the ritual out on the deck that night. The Captain was superstitious and refused to sail in the night, so the only person on deck with her was the man on watch, and he was soon put to sleep. All she'd had to do was offer him a glass of wine with a little belladonna in it. A herb which she kept on her at all times.

With the deck to herself and the stars above, Natalia had drawn with chalk the summoning circle, lit the candles, sketched the runes and letters necessary, and finally, had read the invocation.

The wind whipped into a frenzy, but she observed that the candle flames hardly flickered. The words were bizarre, a language not of this Earth, and she felt a rasp in her throat from the power of them.

The stars above her seemed to grow brighter.

Although her gaze had been fixed on the summoning circle, she chanced a glance up at the sky. The stars were large and closer than she'd ever seen them.

The sight was truly terrifying, but it proved to her that there was real power in what she was doing. In Rupert's name she would see this through.

Her gaze flicked back to the circle to see something there. A silver formless shape, like a cloud caught in the circle, it thrashed, forming eyes and tentacles, then instantly changing again. The thing seemed to be struggling to take form.

She glanced at the book again, scanning quickly to assure herself she hadn't forgotten any part of the invocation.

When she looked up again, she saw a tall man. He was much taller than any man she'd ever encountered before, looked to be almost seven feet tall, and spindly thin as a scarecrow. His eyes were a little too large, a little too bright in the dim candlelight. His skin was as pale as hers, his smile almost skull like.

The stars had gone back to their normal state, and Natalia closed the book and moved closer, a smile spreading over her face.

"Well, hello there," the man said. "To whom do I have the pleasure of speaking?"

"Natalia Harrow," Natalia said. She held our her hand to him, offering him an easy way out of the circle. There was no need to keep him trapped, he was to be her servant after all.

The man took her hand, stepped forward and pressed warm lips to the back of her hand.

"Natalia, it's a pleasure. You may call me Nab, short for Naberus. It is one of my names, and I think, a little easier for your tongue."

"So thoughtful," Natalia said. He stepped elegantly out of the circle and with a gesture, banished all evidence of the ritual itself.

"Now you must tell me what I can do, Natalia, to make all your dreams come true."

Natalia sighed happily.

Everything was going so well.

CHAPTER 10

IN WHICH THE CREW OF THE DEVIL'S WHORE
ENCOUNTER THE CREW OF ANOTHER SHIP

I couldn't believe our luck.

First, I was in Tortuga, looking incredible, with my three lovers.

Second, we had run into Bloody Tate, the second most famous pirate on the seas, after my Captain Lucifer of course.

And third, now it looked like there was bad blood between them and we were about to be in the center of a pirate brawl.

Gabriel and Tate were glaring at each other. Someone at a nearby table hissed "Fight!" But in a soft sort of way, like they didn't want to attract any attention to themself.

Gabriel was tall, but Tate still had a couple of inches on him, and his shoulders were far wider. I glanced at the others at Tate's table. A man with a fantastic hairstyle, dressed in black with a similar amount of flair to Gabriel, the redhead, who looked sort of weirdly familiar, and sitting closest to us, turning to watch, a gorgeous person with a fitted bodice, the kind of thing you might see on a courtly lady, but loose sailor's pants on their bottom half and no shoes. The other man at the table exuded the kind of energy that led you to believe that he could attack at any time. He was eyeing us even more suspiciously than the others.

Gabriel drew his cutlass and Tate drew his sword and they crossed steel with a ringing clang that seemed to echo off the walls.

Then Tate started to laugh, a deep belly laugh of pure joy. Gabriel dropped his cutlass down to his side and grinned flashing Tate a wink. Tate sheathed his sword and clapped Gabriel on the shoulder.

"It's good to see you, old friend."

The room seemed to breathe out collectively, and then people started to talk to each other again, resuming conversations.

I was torn between delight and disappointment. But I settled on delight. "Gabriel knows Bloody Tate?" I turned to Dante for confirmation. He nodded.

"Of course, Captain *Lucifer* does," Dante said. "The seas aren't that big, and the number of safe ports like this one are numbered."

"He never told me that!"

Tate pulled out the chairs of the table adjacent to the one they were seated at and then shoved the tables together to make one big one. "Come on, come join us. I'll buy you dinner, it's the least I can do."

Gabriel took a seat and then turned to gesture us forward.

Dante took a seat next to the man with the pompadour hairstyle with shaved sides. Oliver brushed his shoulder with mine and murmured. "Must be the Shearwater Pirate," and I realised he was right. Another living legend of the seas.

"And the other guy?" I whispered back.

"Don't you recognise the Governor's son?" Oliver said, giving me a mischievous smile.

The Governor's son? Keene? I was supposed to go to some party at their house in Kingston but instead I went to the Hellfire club and got this cursed tattoo on my back. Perhaps I should have done as Father expected and gone there instead...

I took the seat beside Gabriel, and Oliver sat on my other side.

A barmaid brought over a tray with fresh glasses and jugs of ale. Tate asked her to bring them some food as well. Once that was sorted, Gabriel cleared his throat.

"Looks like you have some new recruits..."

"This is Gideon, my boyfriend." *Gideon Keene, that's right. The name rung a bell.* "Thanks to Gideon, we have a sort of bevy of lovers. This is Ora," Tate said, pointing at the person with the stays and the loose pants. "And you remember Ezra, my first mate. And uh, the ship's cat, Zebulon..."

"That's not a cat, that's a man," I said. Tate and the rest of them all turned to look at me. "Uh, sorry, was that impolite?"

Gabriel wrapped his arm around my shoulders rather roughly, which I expect was his way of telling me to be quiet.

"We've actually met before, Gideon," Gabriel said, turning to the Governor's son. "At a all at your father's house. I was looking for this one... This is Cedric Hale-Harrington, my paramour. He's joined my ship, and his boyfriend Oliver." Oliver raised a hand to wave sheepishly at the group, a gentle blush colouring his cheeks.

Gideon narrowed his eyes and leaned forward on his elbows, peering at me. "Your name is terribly familiar to me, Cedric."

"Oh uh, well, your father invited me to a party at your place back in Kingston," I said. "But I didn't go. I had a... uh, prior invitation. I believe our fathers know each other."

"There was talk about you that night," Gideon said, grinning widely. He was weirdly beautiful, there was something about the sharpness of his cheekbones, and the way the lantern light caught in his auburn hair that was very distracting and alluring. "I was sorry not to meet you, but I had business to finish with my father."

"I imagine so."

Gideon smiled and raised his glass to toast me. "It's my pleasure to meet you now."

"Uh, yes, same. And in a far more interesting place than the Governor's house in Kingston."

"Did you say that... you're all lovers of the captain?" Oliver said. The three of us leaned in to confer over the table. Tate and Gabriel turned to talk to each other at the corner and largely ignored us.

Gideon smiled and shrugged a shoulder. "Well, technically they're all *my* lovers, but Tate was my first. And he has a separate boyfriend as well, but he doesn't like crowds too much, so he's still on the Kelpie."

I nodded, impressed. "Good one. Not so much luck with the marrying a nice girl then?"

Gideon shook his head and laughed, a curiously musical sound. "How did you get out here? The last I heard you'd been kidnapped..." he eyed Gabriel.

"I was," I said. "But then we worked it out to the mutual benefit of all the parties involved." Gideon laughed and we clinked our glasses together and drank.

Oliver shook his head at both of us.

"I got Father to write pardons for Tate and Ezra, and we have a letter of marque now," Gideon said, boasting a little.

"Lucifer has a gentleman persona for London," I said, grinning. "So he doesn't need a letter of marque." Gideon and I smiled at each other, something passing warm passing between us.

"I feel like I should separate you two, before something terrible happens," Oliver mumbled.

"Don't be ridiculous, Ollie," I said. "Gideon and I understand each other perfectly, what could possibly go wrong?" I pushed his beer towards him. "Drink up and relax."

Oliver took the mug of beer and drank it agreeably enough.

In the brief silence I heard a snippet of conversation from a nearby table. The words piqued my interest and I leaned back in the chair to listen.

"Some sort of magic light, like a fairy light, maybe. Or some witch up to no good."

"Aye, that's right, green light shooting into the sky. Tall as anything, like it was pointing at the moon," the man said.

"Where'd you say?"

"We thought it was over Saint Vincent," the man said.

"So, are you in town long?" Gideon asked, distracting me from my eavesdropping. Although I thought I'd better mention the green light to Dante all the same.

"Oh uh, I think just a few days," I said. "We're uh, well, it's not good to stay in one place too long."

"I can well understand that," Gideon said. He glanced fondly at Ezra, who, yes, as the Shearwater Pirate, or possibly former Shearwater Pirate, would have been hotly pursued by the authorities. "Although Ezra has a pardon now, thanks to negotiations with my Father, we're still sailing on the noon tide. So, I'm terribly glad we met you now."

I felt a warmth in my chest, seeing Gideon with all these lovers. He made it seem like the most natural thing on Earth, and he clearly had a lot of affection for each of them. I felt a pang of something like envy, and then told myself not to be so ridiculous. I had Oliver, and I had Dante and Gabriel as well, there was nothing to be envious of.

Except perhaps that they all seem devoted to each other, a nasty voice in my head piped up. *And they've made some kind of commitment. You don't know what will happen next week, let alone in the future.*

I crossed my legs and uncrossed them, disliking this new little voice, and the feeling of uncertainty it brought with it.

Oliver shuffled his chair closer to mine, pressing his thigh against my leg. That perked me right up, and I moved closer to put my arm around his shoulders, smiling.

Gabriel waved the waitress down and she brought over some more jugs of ale. I could see that this evening was going to get raucous.

Oliver downed his ale and slammed the mug on the table.

"You want another?" Tate asked, grinning and already pouring it out.

Oliver adjusted his glasses and gamely lifted the mug to his lips. "Fantastic!"

His cheeks were flushed pink and I didn't think it was from my proximity. His eyes seemed to be slower to focus on me than usual.

"You all right?" I asked, leaning closer against him and feeling how hot he was against me.

"Fantastic," he said again. "Maybe a bit tipsy, if I'm being ferpectly...perf... quite honest."

"You're adorable," I said, and kissed his lips. He kissed me back with no hesitation and soon the table was whooping and cheering us on. When we finally came up for air, Gideon was sandwiched between Tate and Ezra, their hands all over each other, and him kissing first one and then the other.

Ora and Zebulon were also tangled together, and Gabriel had an arm around Dante and they were both watching me with interest.

"Perhaps we ought to retire for the night?" Oliver mumbled against my jawline.

"Perhaps we should..." I said, glancing back over at Dante and Gabriel. They were both looking at me rather intensely. "Want me to come and tuck you in? I think I'll be bedding with Gabriel tonight, though..."

Dante kicked me under the table. "Lucifer," he hissed.

I swallowed and blushed, because of course even if these were friends, I had to remember to call Gabriel by his alias in public.

Oliver paused in his nibbling of my neck and then nuzzled in under my ear. My stomach exploded in tingly butterflies.

"I think I'm too drunk to do too much anyway," he murmured. "Come tuck me in."

So, I helped Oliver up to his room, and got him undressed. We kissed for a while, stroking our hands over each other, but in a sort of lazy, indulgent way rather than an urgent one.

I excused myself when he started to yawn, giving him a kiss on the forehead, and then went to find Dante and Gabriel to do something about the state of arousal I found myself in.

CHAPTER 11

IN WHICH LUSTS ARE SLAKED

I let myself into Gabriel's room, locked the door behind me and turned to find the most delightful and inviting view I could have imagined. Gabriel lay back on the pillows, his head tilted back and his chest bare, displaying his fine muscles.

Dante was further down the bed, bent to the work of sucking his cock. I felt my own arousal heighten sharply, and wasted no time in removing my clothes.

Dante paused from his task and looked up at me, his eyes dark with lust.

Gabriel beckoned me closer, raising his head to give me a warm and salacious smile.

"Is young Mister Stanhope well? I had thought he'd be entertaining you," Gabriel said, as if he were enquiring after him in a salon or some similarly formal occasion. Dante leaned in and licked at him.

"Too many sheets to the wind to do anything of the sort," I said. I stepped out of the last of my vestments and sat on the side of the bed. "I imagine he'll have a thumping great regret in the morning."

Gabriel tutted his tongue against his teeth. Then he sat up

slightly, buried a hand in my hair and pulled me in for a rough kiss. I felt his teeth against my lip and moaned, flicking my tongue out to find his and closing my eyes as they tangled together.

"What are you in the mood for, puppy?" Gabriel murmured, his breath hot against my jaw as he kissed his way to my earlobe and bit it.

Groaning, I stroked his chest and tried to catch my breath. "Everything. Anything."

His fingers tightened in my hair and he pulled my head back, exposing my throat so he could bite it.

Imagine, I thought wildly, *if Dante had turned him, and they were both vampires now. Both of them thirsting for my blood, wanting me so badly.*

The thought was so inspiring I nearly orgasmed right then, but I held myself back. Gabriel's bites were possessive, and had nothing to do with feeding, and they ignited heat in my blood that made me want to be closer to him.

"Come on, get in the middle," Gabriel said.

I glanced over my shoulder to see Dante moving off Gabriel's cock, reaching for me. I didn't need any more prompting. I climbed on top of Gabriel, settling myself on my knees so I could grind myself on his slick cock. Gabriel reached for the pot of oil, reached between us and started to tease himself open. That was a surprise, but one I didn't dwell on too much, because Dante had moved in close behind me, wound an arm around my chest and was kissing my shoulder. I could feel his hardness against the small of my back and I reached a hand back to grip his hip and pull him closer.

Dante's free hand dipped into the oil and in a moment I felt his slippery fingers pushing against my hole. Impatient, I rocked my hips back, trying to urge him to move faster and get the thing done so that we could get to the good part. My movement gave Gabriel a little more room to work, and he groaned, capturing my attention. His eyes were half closed, watching the two of us move, and his lower lip was caught between his teeth. Slowly, he hitched one knee up, drawing it from between where I was kneeling, giving me an incredible view of how he was opening himself up with deft fingers.

I couldn't remember him ever taking cock before in this manner, and I wondered briefly, if it meant something. Something emotional, or something about trust perhaps, but then again, perhaps it was a purely practical matter of logistics.

Dante was working me with two fingers, and I felt if we prolonged this too much longer I would simply lose control.

"Gabriel, please," I gasped, thrusting my hips forward to brush my cock against the back of his hand. He withdrew his fingers, wrapped them around my cock, oiling it with three delicious tugs, before guiding me to push against him.

I did so gently, practically shuddering as I held back my need and enthusiasm. This was possibly a one time offer Gabriel was making, and I didn't want to botch it.

Dante's fingers slowed but didn't entirely still as I pushed inside Gabriel. Gabriel's eyes were closed now, one hand guiding me in and the other fisting in the bedclothes as Gabriel moaned loud enough to drown out the noises I was making.

Finally I was deep within him, gasping with the heat and tightness of him.

"Dante, please be quick," I puffed. "I can't hold back for long…"

Dante's fingers withdrew and were replaced with the velvety length of his cock, deliciously hard but smooth and welcome.

Dante's arm around my chest gripped me tighter as he slipped inside, quicker and easier than it had been for me and Gabriel.

Gabriel's eyes were glued to my face, none of the control and domination that I was accustomed to seeing there. Instead he looked open, undone and desperately needy.

"For the love of the Devil's Whore," he croaked. "Fuck me already."

With that kind of prompting I didn't hesitate. I rocked my hips back to bury Dante deeper inside me and then forward to thrust inside Gabriel.

Dante's fingers curled and dug into my chest, igniting sparks of need, and Gabriel's hands found my hips, partially guiding me to move and partially hanging on.

Dante's lips were on my neck, and he moved easily with me as I leaned in to kiss Gabriel's flushed cheeks and suck on his bitten lip. "So beautiful," I murmured. Hardly aware what I was saying except that I wanted him to know how appreciative I was, the words fell from my mouth, urgent and sincere. "You're so incredibly beautiful, Captain. Thank you for everything, you're incredible..."

Dante was thrusting into me from behind and from the noises he was making he was getting close. I closed my fist around Gabriel's cock and began pumping it, whimpering with need as he squeezed and clenched around me. "Yes, that's it just like that," Gabriel groaned.

"Cedric, I'm about to..." Dante whispered in my ear and I nodded, feeling my own body clenching and squeezing in turn.

"Together," I managed to say, in between heavy breaths, and as if we'd rehearsed it the three of us came in the same moment. I felt myself filled with Dante's seed, Gabriel's spilling over my fingers as I tugged him and my own cock throbbing and releasing deep inside him.

I saw stars, and not the frightening kind this time, just the sort that indicated I had enjoyed myself and perhaps needed a little more oxygen.

Dante withdrew, gently pulled me back so I could withdraw from Gabriel, and was cleaning us all up before I could see straight. I settled in the crook of Gabriel's arm, smiling and barely able to open my eyes.

Gabriel pulled me close against him and kissed me again, something urgent and needy in it. I returned it, although I wasn't feeling quite so urgent or needy myself.

Dante settled on Gabriel's other side, smiling at me over his chest when we broke the kiss, and the two of us wrapped Gabriel in our limbs. I let my affection wash over me, and planted little kisses on his collarbone and neck, nuzzling against him until he chuckled.

It felt as if he had given me a gift, and I wanted to thank him for it, but something told me such thanks would only be welcome in non-verbal form.

Dante sat up briefly to extinguish the light, and Gabriel kissed first my forehead and then Dante's.

"You two are going to be the death of me," he said, but the warmth in his tone belied the words.

I kissed the tips of Dante's fingers, where they lay close to my face, and closed my eyes.

"Hopefully not any time soon," I murmured and let myself drift to sleep.

CHAPTER 12

IN WHICH DANTE AND CEDRIC CONSULT A WITCH

*T*he next morning, Dante and I set out in search of a witch. Dante grumbled a little at rising early when Gabriel was apparently planning to sleep for most of the day and was all warm and cuddly.

I felt similarly tempted to stay, in fact it was something of a wrench to extricate myself from Gabriel's side, but the whole entire point of us coming to Tortuga was to find me a witch, so we had to do it.

I dressed down compared to the night before, wearing one of Oliver's soft blue shirts that I'd stolen from him, and my comfortable trousers and boots. I'd asked Oliver if he wanted to accompany us, for scientific, learning about the world reasons, but he'd declined. He had to find a post office and send a letter to his uncle, he'd said. Although privately I suspected he had declined on account of a raging hangover.

Dante was in one of his white shirts and black waistcoats, but it was different to the ones he'd worn the night before. This waistcoat was of a fine velvet and it was tailored to accentuate his slim waist. His trousers were deepest black, and cut perfectly to accentuate his arse and the turn of his calf.

He was eerily pale in the morning sunshine.

"They're usually in the marketplace at Kingston," I said. "Is it the same here? Are we going to see the witch who made you the charm so you can be out in the sun?"

Dante's jaw tightened. "No, Cedric, that witch died many, many years ago."

"Oh, right, sorry," I said. "But the magic keeps going even though they died? I thought there was some kind of rule about that... magic dying with the person." I was aware I was babbling a little, prying into things he probably didn't want to talk about, but my curiosity got the better of me.

Dante pushed his hands into the pockets of his trousers and hummed a little, considering. "It depends on the form of magic, and if it's bound to something other than the person casting the spell," he said. "In this case, as the charm is bound to me, personally, it outlives the witch."

"Oh, so, if you gave the charm to another vampire it wouldn't work the same?

"It would not," Dante said.

I thought about the implications of that for a moment. "Are there a lot of other vampires? I know you said there was a whole group of them in London..."

"All over the place," he said. "Many who prefer to live alone, it can be difficult to find them, and then there are clusters, or broods as we call them, in the bigger cities. London, Paris, Budapest, Marrakech, New York..." he licked his lips and glanced at me. "Why do you want to know?"

I suddenly had the weird thought that he thought I was planning for my future. That I expected him to turn me into a vampire, and I wanted to know what it would be like.

I didn't much like the thought of confusing him, but I wasn't sure about wanting to be a vampire either. Besides, I had bigger and more pressing problems as regards my future.

"Just wondering," I said. "It's rather impressive that you've managed to largely stay hidden. I mean, people generally don't think vampires are real, right?"

"Maybe we can talk about this in private," Dante said. I looked at him and he glanced around, a little nervous. I felt instantly guilty, as if I'd summoned a hoard of vampire hunters down on us, although of course no one seemed to be paying particular attention to us.

"Right, sorry. Um, how do we find a witch?"

"Down here." Dante reached for my hand and led me down an alleyway, past a milliners and a shop that seemed to sell polished sea shells. I wondered if it was a front for something more interesting. Dante appeared to be sniffing the air, and moving quicker. His legs were a bit longer than mine so I had to hurry to keep up, since he wasn't letting go of my hand at all.

We turned down another side street and then another, and I lost track of the direction of the inn, but it wasn't like there was anything to worry about when I was with Dante. If anyone tried to rob us or attack us, he could just eat them.

Finally, he slowed and we approached a purple painted door. The window beside it was painted with the words *Tanith Lavoie*, and there was a large rock on display that opened to show a wealth of purple crystals. There was a little wooden sign hanging over the door showing the symbol of a diamond.

"This place, this is a witch," Dante said with certainty.

"Very nice of them to operate out of a shop with a sign on it and all," I said. I knocked on the purple door and then opened it, stepping inside. The room was pleasantly lit with a multitude of candles on shelves around the walls.

There was a large table in the middle of the room, laden with shallow bowls of small stones, or maybe they were gems? Each bowl held a different colour of stone, and I was particularly drawn to some rod shaped ones of a cloudy grey.

"Perhaps it's best if you don't touch anything," a voice came from the back of the room. My hand froze in midair and Dante tutted his tongue against his teeth.

"Miss? Tanith Lavoie, I presume?" he said.

"Not a miss, nor a mister. Just Tanith."

I looked in the direction of the voice and saw a tall person with broad shoulders, a heart shaped face and a floor length grey robe. They had long, black hair tied into a braid that sat over one shoulder.

"My name is Tanith, how can I help you..." they said. It sounded like it was supposed to be a question but their tone didn't rise up at the end at all.

Dante moved closer behind me, I turned towards the witch, Tanith, and cleared my throat.

"Hi, hello, I'm a bit cursed, and I was wondering if you could help out with that."

"Depends on the curse, and what 'a bit cursed' means," Tanith rolled their eyes. "And to be honest, curse breaking isn't exactly my forté. But I'll take a look, assuming you can pay."

"Yes, I can pay," I said quickly, then remembered that witches didn't always want payment with money. "I mean, assuming you want payment in coin rather than something like blood."

"Coin is fine." Tanith beckoned to me and I walked closer, Dante following close behind. They looked up at him and rolled their eyes. "It's all right, Day Walker, I'm not going to hurt him."

Dante hissed a little. "Don't call me that."

"Denial will not change what you are."

"Just call me Dante," he grumbled.

Between the two of them I felt like the one cheerful person in the world. Tanith took my hand and looked into my eyes. "Okay, well, tell me all about it."

"Uh, there's a tattoo on my back, and it gives me nightmares and some cult is trying to use me to bring an ancient god... monster... into this world? And I guess that will kill me when it happens?" I said, trying to sum it up as best I could.

Tanith's eyes widened and they dropped my hand.

"What cult?"

"Uh, the cult of the Unknowable Way?"

Tanith swore, bustled past me and Dante to the front of the shop and locked the door. "Oh I hate those idiotic white nobles so much. You'd better come in the back, I guess. I don't know that I can remove the curse, but I can probably do something to help."

"You've heard of them, then?" I asked.

"Well, yes, I mean, they're causing ripples all through the magical world," Tanith said. They gestured to the back of the shop, where there was a beaded curtain hanging down. "Go through there, and you'd better show me this tattoo."

I glanced at Dante, feeling a little nervous about their reaction. He nodded encouragingly and kind of shrugged. I took this to mean "whatever happens I'll protect you", which was very comforting.

I walked through into what appeared to be Tanith's kitchen. There was a kettle on the hob, and a small dining table in front of a merrily burning fire. Considering the heat outside, it ought to have been stifling in there, but somehow it just felt pleasantly warm. Magic, I supposed.

Dante leaned in the corner, watching the room, sort of like a guard dog. If a guard dog was a cranky bat. A six foot tall cranky bat.

Tanith followed me in, their fingers rubbing their small pink crystal pendant. They nodded to me and I started to unbutton Oliver's shirt, shrugged it off my shoulders. Although their words weren't exactly hostile, I got the distinct impression that Tanith was annoyed with me.

I pulled the shirt all the way off and turned so my back was to Tanith.

"So you've heard of the cult?"

"Yes, and I had hoped I wouldn't have to hear of them again.

Nasty, foolish business they're wrapped up in, the books document it going back hundreds of years. I'd heard rumours that the latest resurgence was just a bunch of rich white people making fools of themselves."

"It might have started out that way," I said. "But then they tried to sacrifice me."

They sighed deeply. "This is... yes, all right this is very serious."

My stomach formed a hard knot and my mouth went dry. I mean, obviously I had known it was serious. I knew that, but hearing it said by a witch I'd gone to for help made it a lot worse, somehow.

I swallowed a lump in my throat and gritted my teeth together.

"Is there any way to remove it?" Dante asked. From his voice it sounded as if he'd come closer, but I stared fixedly at the wall so I didn't just start blubbering and begging for help.

Tanith made a non-committal sound. "I don't know about removing it... the spell that put it on there must've been strong... and really, my speciality is crystals, which are good for a lot of things but body modification isn't one of them." I took a deep and somewhat ragged breath. "But I'll see what I can do. I might need to call up a whole coven, and that will take a day or two, so..."

I felt a soft, warm finger tracing the pattern over my back. The pattern was quite familiar to me by now.

"What can you tell me about it?" they asked, their voice a little softer, a little kinder than before. The lump in my throat inexplicably got bigger.

"Uh, the tattoo? I don't remember it being done. I must've... passed out or something."

"Or been drugged," Dante suggested, which didn't exactly make me feel better.

"Right. I woke up in the morning..." I thought back, trying to remember. "And my back hurt, I thought maybe I'd had a whipping."

"Well, sure," Tanith said, dryly.

"And then... well, uh, I guess it's given me dreams, and then when they caught me in Casablanca, they put this oil on it that seemed to, I don't know. Activate it?"

Tanith sniffed. "They caught you. But you got away."

"Because of Dante." I turned then to look over my shoulder at him. "Well, the whole crew of the ship I'm a... crew member on. Sort of."

"Well, it sounds like you have some decent luck on your side, as well as some very good friends," Tanith said. They bustled away and started opening tiny drawers, pulling out bits and pieces from several of them and placing them in a shallow dish.

"And then there's the... token." Dante said. "You should probably tell them about the token."

"Oh, yes, the dreams got worse and I woke up with a weird thing in my hand. It was in the dream, and then I had it in my hand."

"What's it look like?"

Tanith paused in their work, looking at me. I opened my mouth to describe it, when I became aware that there was a familiar weight in my pocket.

It can't be. It was in the safe. It was hidden from me, I thought. *I didn't put it in my pocket this morning, I'm sure of it. I...*

I stuck my hand into my pocket and drew out the small wooden figure, holding it out on my palm so Tanith could see it. I felt cold.

Dante pushed off from the wall to peer at it. "I thought we left it on the ship?"

"I thought we did, too."

Tanith leaned over my hand, but didn't make any move to touch it. "That's... yes, that's very bad, Cedric."

"Fuck." My voice broke on it, and the cold gave way to unpleasant trembles. "Dante."

He put his hand around my shoulders and kissed the top of my head. "We're getting you help."

"Yeah, I'm going to need a coven for this," Tanith said. They went back to their dish of small crystals and tipped them into a small woven bag and pulled the strings tight, whispering a couple of words of power over the bundle. I put my shirt back on as they worked. "This should work as a stop gap, it'll ease the dreams for a bit. It's a combination of clear quartz, hematite, black tourmaline, it's powerful."

They offered me the bag and I took it in my free hand. "Should I... put the thingie in there?" I gestured the wooden figure towards the bag, but they shook their head.

"No. But keep the bag on you."

"Should I try burning it?"

Tanith folded their arms. "I doubt you'll be able to get rid of it, even if you were to burn it or cast it into the deepest part of the ocean. Until the curse or spell is lifted, this thing will be connected to you and it will find its way back, I think."

"Thank you," Dante said, before I could. "What do we owe you?"

"Just a couple of silver pieces for now," Tanith said. "Where are you staying?"

"The Pickled Oyster," Dante said. I stuffed the bag of crystals down the front of my shirt and pulled out my purse, eager to pay the witch for their help. "Ask for Dante Grigorias. How long will it take you to summon a coven, do you think?"

Tanith shrugged, and accepted the silver from me. "Could be overnight, could be days. It depends what everyone has on, frankly. Don't just shove it in your shirt, though, keep it safe."

I sheepishly pulled it out and pocketed it instead, putting the wooden figure in the pocket on my other hip.

"Really, thank you so much," I said. Tanith gave me the

barest glimpse of a smile and then nodded back at the door to the main shop.

"I'll be in touch. Good luck. Last I heard the cult of the Unknowable Way steered clear of Tortuga port, so you don't have to worry too much about being jumped. Well, just the normal amount for a place as full of thieves and pirates as this is."

I smiled, feeling a weight lift that I wasn't aware I'd been carrying. "Really, thank you."

Tanith saw us out of the shop, and when we stepped out into the late morning sunshine I felt the knot in my stomach resolve itself into hope.

Dante offered me his arm and I took it gladly. We strolled back to the Oyster in a slow, meandering way, Dante showing me the sights of a town he knew very well indeed.

CHAPTER 13

IN WHICH CHANGES ARE NOTED

*B*y their third night in Tortuga, Gabriel heard four different retellings of a weird green light that had been spotted on the island of Saint Vincent. He was sitting out on the verandah of the Pickled Oyster, enjoying the warm night air and nursing a glass of fine whiskey on his own.

It was unusual that people were talking so much about one incident, which meant that it wasn't just sea folk exaggerating and telling tall tales. In fact the details of each time he'd heard it told barely varied.

The people who'd seen it were spooked. These were fearsome pirates, privateers and mercenaries... and they'd seen a weird magic they couldn't explain or understand.

And Gabriel had the uncomfortable feeling that it had happened on the same night as Cedric's last bad nightmare.

Thankfully, Cedric's sleep had been undisturbed since the witch he'd visited had cast her spell. Cedric's new charm appeared to be doing what it was supposed to.

Gabriel loved it on Tortuga. He didn't have to pretend to *be* anything here, he could just relax, enjoy some good food, fine ale and the company of his favourite people.

Because, although he had always had a certain affection for

the men in his crew, something about Cedric's presence, his warmth and easy way of laughing about things had brought out more... tenderness, perhaps, in Gabriel's own emotions.

And besides that he was never short on someone to warm his bed. Cedric was more than willing, and Dante as well.

He wondered, idly, why he had never considered Dante as an option previously, especially when their friendship had so easily and naturally grown into something more. He felt an attachment there which, in retrospect, he could have acted on sooner. But he didn't like regretting past choices he'd made. The past was the past, and there was nothing to be done about it.

Their rooms at the Pickled Oyster were comfortable, the food was good, and it did the crew good to have some time on land, some leave to do as they liked. And his crew were loyal enough that he knew the ship would be safe and secure the entire time.

However, the green light story was of some concern. He downed his whiskey and resolved to find Dante and talk to him about it. If there was magic afoot it could bode poorly for his crew, his ship, and of course, Cedric. And Gabriel's protectiveness of the boy had only grown in the last few weeks. Although he felt he needed more time in Tortuga, the green light might mean they had to weigh anchor earlier than planned. Whatever he had to do to keep Cedric out of the hands of the blasted cult.

Inside, the Pickled Oyster was as busy as usual, and Gabriel knew that Cedric was at a table in there, beguiling Oliver with some kind of story, no doubt about himself and the many and varied trials he'd been through.

Dante had gone for a walk in the dark streets, and Gabriel suspected he was talking to some locals of his persuasion, and thought it best not to ask questions of him when he came back. Some things it was better not to pry into.

He finished his whiskey and sighed, stretching his arms up over his head. Perhaps he ought to join Cedric and Oliver?

Oliver had been an interesting influence on Cedric. He hadn't calmed him down, Cedric was still utterly insatiable and forward with his desires. But he seemed to be attentive to Oliver, which was somewhat touching. It was a side of Cedric he hadn't seen before they'd taken Oliver on board. He paid attention to Oliver, instead of just himself.

Which wasn't exactly fair, Cedric was generous with his attention, especially when it came to the bedroom, but day to day he was a little self-centred. Or at least, he pretended to be. Gabriel wasn't at all sure that it wasn't an act he put on, but the truth of that would take time to reveal. He'd have to be patient if he wanted to know the true Cedric. And he did want to, he was surprised to admit, even if it was just to himself.

He was aware that they'd stolen this time together, duped his parents to get a little freedom for Cedric. Gabriel knew it was only a matter of time before Cedric's father insisted he settle down, find a wife, lead a respectable life. Whatever they shared together, he couldn't see how it could last.

But perhaps Oliver and Cedric could have an arrangement back in London.

Oliver himself was a delightful blend of buttoned down and mischievous, and Gabriel looked forward to the night when Oliver would consent to joining Cedric and himself in bed. He had no doubt the boy would be a lot of fun.

And fun was what Tortuga was about. It was why it existed, as far as Gabriel was concerned. Gabriel had a plan for his own life, after all. One that included amassing a great amount of coin and retiring somewhere with pleasant weather. He had never assumed he would have a spouse in this picturesque future, if indeed he could survive long enough to enjoy it. No, he had imagined buying some kind of Knighthood and one of those glorious manor houses in the English countryside and seeing out his days in peace. He had no desire for a wife, after all, and it would be all sorts of scandal to have a man live with him.

He sighed and propped his feet up on another chair and laughed quietly at himself for dreaming of a future that might never be. It didn't pay to lose oneself in a dream, after all. It was far better to enjoy the present.

As he sipped the whiskey, he heard Cedric's unmistakable laugh... wild and infectious, and smiled a little.

Maybe once Cedric had seen the witches for this special spell, he'd suggest something... something Oliver, Cedric and himself could all enjoy. Something rough and hot that would leave them with marks in the morning.

But for now, for this moment, he'd enjoy the peace and quiet, and the last of the whiskey.

CHAPTER 14

IN WHICH A COVEN OF WITCHES PERFORMS
A RITUAL

I'd just polished off a large and frankly delicious breakfast of bacon, eggs, and buttered toast when a girl of about twelve came looking for me.

I'd been enjoying the food at the Pickled Oyster immensely. On this particular morning I was dining with Bilal. Oliver had gone off in the early morning to examine some rare orchid or something dreadfully boring and *Oliver*ish. Gabriel had continued to snore stubbornly and Dante didn't really eat that much in the first place, so had begged off breakfast to lie in a while longer.

Bilal was good company, they were quite content to listen to me talk, and they had the same passion for the bread this place made as I did. I was telling Bilal all about life back in London when both of us noticed the little girl walking in.

She went to the bar, striding up to it like she owned the place, and spoke to the barmaid, whose name was Delphine. I was watching because it was sort of bizarre to see a little girl here in Tortuga at all, let alone striding into the tavern, even if it was breakfast time and generally devoid of drunken shenanigans.

The barmaid pointed over at me, and the girl came hurtling over.

"Dante Girgorias?" she asked.

I shook my head. "No, I'm Cedric. Did Tanith send you?"

She nodded. "They're all gathering now, from all over. Tanith said to be at her shop at midday, err... please, because that's the most fortuitous time to make the magic."

I dug a coin out of my purse and tossed it to the girl. "Then I'll be there at midday, thanks for your trouble."

She caught it and beamed, revealing the cheekiest dimples I'd ever seen, and a missing tooth. "Thanks, Cedric!"

Then she turned and bounded off. No doubt to spend the coin on sweetmeats or ribbons. Or, well, she worked for a witch, possibly she was going to purchase a pet toad.

"You ought to be careful, giving your name out so readily," Bilal said.

"Maybe." I shrugged and finished the last bit of toast. "But the witches are assembled, and they're going to remove my tattoo, maybe... I don't care a fig about anything else. If they get the tattoo off me, the cult won't want me any more and all my problems are solved!"

Bilal nodded and squeezed my hand, unexpectedly. I gave them a lopsided smile. "Well, let's hope they can do it then."

Dante insisted on accompanying me to Tanith's, although I told him I didn't feel I needed an escort.

"Really, it's a place I've been before, it will fine," I said.

"Perhaps I should come too," Gabriel said. He'd woken up but hadn't left the bed, he was propped up on the pillows, reading a book, his bare chest exposed. He looked delightfully inviting and if it had been any other kind of appointment I would have missed it to stay in bed with him and lick every inch of his skin. But this was too important to get side-tracked.

"You know, there could be robbers, or cultists, or kidnappers..."

"I can take care of him," Dante replied.

"I can take care of myself!"

"Well, take a sword at least, pup." Gabriel said.

I strapped on a rapier that Gabriel had brought ashore, although I didn't tell him that I wasn't sure I'd have much stomach to actually use it on anyone. It didn't matter, I'd have Dante with me, and there was no one in my mind more ferocious.

"And you're quite sure these are trustworthy witches?" Gabriel said, eyeing Dante.

"Certain," Dante said. "I've asked around, and from what I can tell from my friends and acquaintances, no one would allow the Cult of Unknowable Way to linger on this island."

"Hm." Gabriel nodded. "Perhaps we ought to linger here longer..."

"We'd best be going if we're to be there at midday," I said, and tugged Dante out of the room.

I had a bounce in my step as I walked to Tanith's. It was a lovely morning, the breeze carrying the smell of the ocean, and the sunlight pouring warmth down on us.

"You're particularly sunshiney today," Dante observed. He had produced a pair of spectacles with blue tinted lenses that he slipped on. It made him look a little more eccentric than normal, but delightfully intriguing at the same time.

"And why shouldn't I be? I'm out with one of my favourite men, and I'm about to have a curse lifted off me."

Dante's hair was brushed and pulled back in a low ponytail and he wore a light linen shirt with a black waistcoat, black trousers and boots. I was tempted to go and buy him a sword cane to complete the look.

I had stolen another of Oliver's shirts because, besides the fact that they smelled of him, they were lovely and soft against my skin.

The walk to the witch's shop was pleasant and uneventful

and I allowed myself to feel bright and hopeful, walking alongside my vampiric lover.

Tanith's had a sign on the door "Closed for private function".

I knocked on the door and then tried the handle. The door wasn't locked. I peered in and called out. "Hello?"

"In the back!" Tanith's voice rang out. I could hear other voices as well, there seemed to be quite a group gathered.

Dante followed me in and we made our way to the back. The room was empty and the back door stood open, letting the sunlight in. There was a group of people gathered in the small courtyard that the store backed onto.

They all turned to look at me and Dante, so I raised my hand, gave them all a winning smile and waved. "Hello there!"

Tanith came forward and took both my hands, drawing me into to the centre of the courtyard. The ground was packed dirt, dry and dusty, but they'd obviously spent some time with paint and brush, because there was an elegant symbol decorating the yard. The whole set up felt horribly familiar.

"Into the middle there, Cedric," Tanith said. "And Dante can hold your shirt. We'll need to put some powders and things on your back."

"Sorry, before I do that," I said, clearing my throat. "Can I just ask what it is you're going to do here?"

"A spell of binding, not of you but of the curse," Tanith said. "I thought that was clear."

"Right, but the actual... ritual. You're not going to rub my back with special oil or summon a dark being with my blood?"

"No blood magic," Tanith said, seeming to understand my line of questioning now. "Some crystals, some pastes and potions, but nothing that will activate the tattoo. We will burn some herbs and bind the curse. It won't hurt at all. Now, please, remove your shirt so we can get started while the sun is at its zenith."

"Oh, sure." I stayed where they'd guided me and unbuttoned the shirt, tossing it to Dante, who seemed reluctant to step onto the symbol on the ground.

"Hello, love," a tall and impressive woman said. She was wearing a flowing robe that shimmered with blues and purples. "I'm Adianez, nice to meet you."

"Nice to meet you too," I said.

"Now, close your eyes for a moment, will you?"

"Uh, sure," I did as she asked. In a moment I felt something cool and wet dabbed on my eyelids. "What does this do?"

"Sometimes we need a little help to truly see," she said. I felt her blow over my eyelids, presumably to dry off whatever she'd put on me. "You've seen more than we have, with regards to these people and their spells. It may help us. There now, you can open your eyes." She smiled at me and stepped around behind me.

I tried my absolute best not to fidget as she daubed my back with something damp. My tattoo didn't respond to the concoction, which I hadn't realised I was worried about until she was done and the skin of my back just felt like skin with stuff put on it. She moved away and took a glass jar from Tanith, smearing a little of what was on her fingers inside of it.

A man with a startlingly bright green, marvellously bushy moustache and full beard approached me next.

He had sparkling eyes that I instantly liked, looking at me over some semi-circle spectacles. In his hand he had a smouldering bundle of herbs tied together with string. It was giving off a generous amount of thick white smoke and he waved it around my head, filling the air around me.

"Is it all right if I breathe that in?" I asked, since it seemed inevitable that I would.

"Of course, son, in fact, it's best if you do."

I inhaled the smoke. It was sweet, acrid, like a very intense incense. It filled my throat and then lungs and made me cough.

The witch hummed and waved the smoking stick up and down my body, no doubt infusing the smell indelibly into my clothes. But I shrugged off this little irritation.

They are trying to help me, so there's no sense worrying about what my clothes will smell like at the end of it.

"Step aside, Bretton," a woman's voice said. "He needs some rue now."

"All right, Brinna, all right." The man, Bretton, stepped back, and a woman who had to be his sibling, or possibly a twin, stepped forward. Her hair had streaks of the same green as his moustache in it, and their faces looked very similar indeed.

Bretton held his slowly burning bundle out and Brinna pressed a leafy sprig of something green against it, until the leaves began to smoke.

"Breathe this in too, son," she said. "Rue is powerful."

"Sure," I murmured, although my eyes were watering now. I swallowed another cough and breathed in again, trying to do it slowly and carefully without choking on it. It wasn't terribly easy.

It was strange to think of these people doing all this magic on me, and not feeling afraid at all. Unlike the cult, who had tied me down and done things without asking, this group were kind, gentle, and far more inclined to explain what they were doing. I could feel the magical power, making the air quiver, but my tattoo wasn't responding, and I felt secure. Dante was only a few yards away, watching all the proceedings, which was also a comfort.

My eyes watered, irritated from the smoke and the strange sensation of magic around me. I blinked rapidly, trying to clear my eyes.

Finally, Brinna and Bretton backed away with their herbal smoke and I gratefully drew a lungful of fresh air. My mouth felt dry and my head a little light.

I wiped my eyes on the back of my wrist as Tanith walked

forward with another witch. Behind them, Bretton and Brinna extinguished their herbs and crumbled the remains into the same jar Adianez had used.

"More black tourmaline," Tanith said. They pulled out a bundle, unwrapped it and showed me a black crystal, resting on the cloth it had been wrapped in. "Take it with your bare hand. It's been cleansed, so it will imprint on you, right now."

"Imprint?"

"Attach itself to you. In a sense, it will understand it's yours."

"Oh, lovely, thank you." I took the crystal and cradled it in my palm. It felt cool and it fit pleasingly in my hand. I liked the way it felt, for some reason. Almost how the wooden token felt, but not nearly as frightening to hold. It warmed my palm, even though it was cool to the touch.

"Do you have that little wooden effigy from your dream?" Tanith asked. I dug in my pocket and pulled it out with my free hand. They brought the jar closer and I slipped the wooden figure inside it. It was almost too tall to fit inside it, and some part of me wanted to snatch it back, but I resisted. This was right.

"And now we'll call on the cardinal directions." Tanith turned away, calling to the other witches.

They led the chant and the others joined in, apparently they all knew the words. I tried to hum along quietly.

"We invoke the guardians of the East. The rising sun, please bring illumination, those who pursue this boy hide in the shadows. As the wind blows, let them be revealed to those who would defeat them.

"We invoke the guardians of the South, the noon day sun, that we conjure beneath. Give him courage and protect him against the Cult of the Unknowable Way. Please hide him from their eyes.

"We invoke the guardians of the West, where the sun sets.

Grant introspection and self-awareness, that this boy not take the evil further inside, but be watchful against the corruption.

"We invoke the guardians of the North. Give us your wisdom and allow this cult to be exposed. In your place of mystery, where dreams begin, assist us this day to guard his dreams against evil."

Then Brinna rang a small brass bell. The sound of it seemed impossibly loud, carrying through the ear, echoing back around the yard and reverberating through my bones. It should have felt bizarre, or painful, but it was actually comforting somehow.

Tanith held out the jar, which was filled with the wooden figure, ashes, some herbs, and potions, and handed it to me.

"Put the crystal in here, Cedric."

Reluctantly, I dropped the crystal into the jar. Tanith produced a lid and sealed the jar as the last ringing notes of the bell faded away.

It seemed to be sealing some of the sound inside.

Bretton brought forward a lit black candle and dripped wax around the edge of the jar as Tanith turned it in their hands.

Once they were done, they lifted their head and called out. "So mote it be!"

The other witches repeated the phrase back to them, so I did too.

Then they brought me the jar.

"There, keep that with you."

"Thank you," I said as I took it. It was a small jar, but it wasn't exactly something I could wear around my neck or keep in my pocket. Maybe I could get a little bag for it, or... "How close do I have to keep it?"

"Close as you can manage," Tanith said.

I wanted to say something dry and witty in response to the vagueness of their reply, but I bit my lip. *Never anger a witch, especially one who has gone out of their way to help you.*

I nodded. "Right, thank you, really. What do I owe you?"

Tanith shook their head. "That cult has terrible plans and we don't want those to come to fruition. Besides, a member of the same cult tried to interfere with my business seventy or so years ago. Your payment from earlier will be sufficient. If you can stop the cult from doing what they're planning to do then all the better."

Seventy years ago? But Tanith didn't look older than thirty... I hadn't realised witches lived longer or didn't age. Oliver will be so interested!

"That's... that's more than fair, thank you." I swallowed the dry smokey taste in my mouth and smiled.

"We haven't removed the tattoo, but they shouldn't be able to get to you through it," Tanith said. They squeezed my shoulder and I nodded.

"You've already done so much, thank you, really."

Dante moved forward and we spent a little time expressing our gratitude to each of them. Finally, we made our excuses and walked back to the inn.

CHAPTER 15

IN WHICH THE TUTOR AND THE CAPTAIN
GIVE CEDRIC A SCHOOLING

"So the witches made a powerful protection spell and you should be able to sleep unhaunted now?" Gabriel said, smiling. He had dressed and moved down into the main tavern, and when Dante and I returned we joined him.

"That's what they said," I said. I rolled my shoulders and took Gabriel's drink, downing a few mouthfuls before he took it back off me.

"Order your own, you bad puppy."

I laughed and went to the bar, ordered two drinks for each of us.

While I was up at the bar, who should swan in through the front door but Oliver. He looked incredible, his skin practically glowing with health. His eyes bright behind his spectacles.

"I'll bring it to your table," Delphine said. I gave her a wink and smile and went to greet Oliver.

"Where have you been all day, Mister Stanhope?"

"All over. I've been learning so much," he said. "The orchid was just incredible, and I met a couple of other scientists."

"Well, the witches did their ritual today," I said, bouncing on the balls of my feet.

"They did? Oh, I'm so disappointed I missed it," Oliver sighed and then shook his head. "Well, did it work, did they remove the curse?" His eyes flicked from my face to my shoulder, hopeful.

"They couldn't get rid of the tattoo, but they gave me a jar and it all felt really good."

"They gave you a jar?"

"Yes, there was a whole thing. Do you want to know the details?" I offered, but I felt my nose scrunching as I spoke. I didn't really want to recount the whole entire thing for him, even if he was looking eager and interested. "Maybe tomorrow."

"Good." He grinned, and rocked forward and back like he wanted to hug me but was too nervous. I hugged him instead.

"It's very good. Come on, we're drinking." We got to the table as Delphine finished unloading tankards onto the table.

Later, after a pleasant few hours of drinking, eating and chatting Gabriel started to look at me with a certain intention. He had, I had noticed, called me puppy at least twice more, and it had an effect each time.

He was also observing how closely I was sitting to Oliver and, if I wasn't mistaken, he was eyeing Oliver up as well.

I started to get a certain tingling in my nethers.

The table we occupied now had a few more of the crew of the Whore at it, and was getting noisier by the moment, matching the general roar of the busy tavern. Dante had excused himself to check in with some local vampire or other. He seemed to have quite the web of connections, which I guessed made sense seeing as he must be frightfully old and well travelled. But Dante wasn't the focus of my thoughts.

"I think the captain is planning something," I murmured to Oliver.

Oliver, who had largely been drinking coconut water instead of beer, licked his lips. "What is he planning, do you think?"

"I think there's only one way to find out." I leaned over the table suavely, the effect ruined only slightly when I accidentally rested my elbow in a puddle of spilled beer, and gave Gabriel the eye. "You keep looking at me, Captain Lucifer."

"I admit that I do." Gabriel finished his glass of whiskey and smirked at me.

"Well, what do you want?"

"I was wondering if your Mister Stanhope might like to join us in my room," he said, his voice low, gravelly, but somehow carrying under the noise the others were making.

My cock instantly stiffened and I swallowed hard. I hardly dared to hope. I could feel Oliver's hand on the small of my back, so I eased back into my chair and leaned against his shoulder. "Gabriel's extending an invitation to you, to join him and me, uh, me and him, tonight. If you'd like to."

"Would that be something you'd like, Cedric?" he said, leaning in a bit closer to me. I could see his cheeks were flushed a little pinker than normal, and I wasn't sure if it was because the room was a little stuffy or because the suggestion was such a good one.

I nodded enthusiastically. "Absolutely fuck yes, please and thank you."

"Language," Oliver chuckled. Then I got a front row seat of him looking over to Gabriel with a lascivious look I hadn't known he was capable of. He communicated with his eyebrows that yes, he was in and maybe we ought to go up to the room right then. It was damn suave, which wasn't something I necessarily associated with Oliver. Of course, he wasn't an innocent, I knew that, but he'd always been so buttoned down around me back in Kingston.

He picked up his satchel and stood and I followed him. Gabriel stretched lazily, then excused himself from the table.

"Have fun!" Marco called, giving me a salacious wink.

"I intend to," I fired back.

Then I turned and hurried, because Gabriel and Oliver were already at the stairs.

They seemed to be conferring with each other, bending their heads in. I felt a thrill of anticipation at what they could possibly be talking about. I assumed it was me... which was both intriguing and a little nerve wracking. I both wanted to know what they were saying and wanted a surprise.

They were moving fast, Gabriel's long legs eating up the stairs and Oliver seeming to have no trouble in keeping pace with him. I wasn't about to get out of breath running to follow them, so I walked briskly but didn't hurry.

Once inside Gabriel's room, they were conferring softly between them.

My heart sped up and I licked my lips, closing the door behind me. "Should I ... uh, what should I do?"

Oliver looked over at me with a smile of utter delight but his eyes were full of a very wicked promise that made my dick throb.

"Look at that, he's asking what he should do."

"I told you, he can be very obedient when he's given the right encouragement," Gabriel said to Oliver.

"I find that very hard to believe," Oliver replied. I started to feel a little irritated that they were speaking as if I couldn't talk, or as if I weren't even there. They were *supposed* to be lavishing me with attention after all.

I folded my arms. "If you're just going to talk about me then I'll leave you to it."

"Puppy," Gabriel said, giving me the intense, quelling look that always made my bones feel sort of liquid. "You aren't to speak unless you're spoken to. And we are not ignoring you. Over here." He clicked his fingers and pointed at the floor beside the bed.

Part of me wanted to resist, to stay exactly where I was to

make him come to me, touch me, kiss me. But a bigger part of me wanted to be good and enjoy whatever they had in mind.

I'll be a brat next time.

But I'd apparently already hesitated too long and Gabriel growled low in his throat. He stalked towards me and grabbed me by the collar of my shirt.

"I gave you an order, pup." He turned and pulled, leading me to the spot he'd indicated. "Your tutor here has mentioned a desire to discipline you, puppy. What do you think of that?"

"I... well, I think it's probably rather overdue?" It had meant to be a quip but Gabriel's forcefulness had made me feel a little off footed. I flushed.

Oliver had a bag of Gabriel's and was sorting through it, finally withdrawing a coil of rope. My skin flushed warm. Gabriel still had hold of my shirt, and I felt the need to once again make a quip, but when I opened my mouth nothing came out.

"You want to tie him up first?" Gabriel said. Oliver shook his head, passed him the rope and then took off his glasses, setting them on the side table before approaching us.

"No, I want to put him over my knee and spank him, the way I've been imagining since the first week I met him."

My mouth was dry and my mind was empty of everything, except for question marks. I knew I'd fantasised about him but Oliver had never given me any reason to suspect he felt similarly.

Gabriel propelled me towards Oliver, who caught me by the shoulders and kissed me, further melting my brain into pure desire. I kissed him back with all the longing and arousal I was feeling.

"What do you want, Cedric?"

I inhaled, feeling my cheeks burn. "For you to do whatever you want. Discipline me, please."

He looked me in the eyes for a long moment and then

smiled. "And tell me how you'll let me know if you don't like something one of us is doing? It's fine to say do whatever you want, but I want you to enjoy this... to a degree."

"I'll say stop," I said, promptly. "If there's anything, but I don't think there will be because-"

Without warning, he pulled back, his hand fisted in my shirt, and sat on the edge of the bed, pulling me down.

"Lay over my lap, Cedric," he ordered.

I'd dreamed of this, thought it could never possibly happen, but yearned about it even still.

Just have to do one thing before we get started.

I pulled the witch's jar out of my pocket and set it safely on the table beside the bed.

Then, I draped myself over his knees and found myself staring at the floor. My arms hung down awkwardly, my fingers on the wooden floor.

"How long did you say you've imagined this?" I asked.

Oliver's hand clapped against my ass with a sharp smack.

The air went out of my lungs and I squirmed, some instinct in me wanting to get away, even though my cock and my heart wanted to take whatever Oliver gave me.

Oliver's other hand closed on the back of my neck and pushed my head down, stopping the way I wanted to rear up at the spanks. I moaned as wantonly as any bride on her wedding night.

"That's right," Oliver said, with so much self-satisfaction and veiled venom that my cock strained against my pants. I rocked my hips, trying to get some friction off rutting on his leg. He spanked me again with his palm, the smack seemed to echo around the room. I moaned even louder. Oliver followed it up with three more of the same force.

"It might be more effective, if you expose him," Gabriel said. I had almost forgotten he was in the room. I felt his hands on my waist, pulling my trousers open and then down around my knees. Oliver's hand connected with the bare, and already warmed skin of my ass and I cried out, partly with surprise but the pain had quickly turned into delicious pleasure.

"Yes, you see the difference," Gabriel said.

"Indeed, I was going to get there soon," Oliver said. They actually sounded like they were discussing naval tactics, or some new species of fish.

I was about to protest that they focus on the task at hand, which was, of course, me, when I felt another smack.

The flat of Oliver's palm on my bare skin stung in the first instant, but the heat of it spread through my skin and then up my spine. At the same time it tightened my balls and made my cock throb. I was finding it a little hard to catch my breath, but in the best possible way.

"There now," Oliver said, a few strikes later. "How do you feel, Cedric? Do you feel like you've been adequately punished for all the ways you frustrated me? All the ways you flaunted yourself and your promiscuous ways?"

I swallowed. "Not... not exactly."

Gabriel chuckled darkly and I felt his hand in my hair, pulling. Oliver's hand moved from the back of my neck and the two men hauled me back up to my feet. Both of them made quick work of stripping the rest of my clothes off.

"You don't feel you've atoned enough?" Gabriel asked, his voice arch.

"Uh, no, I didn't mean that," I said. My impetuous courage fading in the face of Gabriel's dominant aura of power.

"One." Gabriel put his finger on my lips and I kissed it gently. It stayed in place. "You will call me Captain, and Oliver Sir, when you address us. If you understand me, nod your head."

I nodded gently, trying not to dislodge his finger. "Good boy. Now, the second rule is that you mustn't lie to either of us. Now,

I'm going to ask you again, and this time you will answer me honestly. Do you think you've been punished enough?"

"No, Captain," I said quickly, then swallowed before answering. "No, I've yearned for Oliver to correct me for quite some time. And, and all that was absolutely divine and I want more. Please." I added the please belatedly.

Oliver's hand slapped my ass hard and I gasped. "Call me Sir, Cedric."

"Sorry, Sir."

"Hands in front of you, puppy." He started to uncoil the rope and I felt tingles shoot through me. I lifted my arms, although there wasn't exactly a lot of space between me and Gabriel. I felt Oliver move closer behind me, he'd undressed while I spoke to Gabriel. He pressed his body against my back, his hand moved around my waist and I groaned, feeling the skin of my arse smarting where it was pressed against his hips. His cock pressed against me and I groaned again.

Gabriel lashed my wrists together, looping the rope multiple times around my lower arms, then tying it off securely. Then he kissed me, and I realised I'd been wanting him all day. When I'd been getting ready to leave that morning he'd looked so inviting, lounging in the bed. I showed my appreciation by sucking on his tongue, which tasted deliciously smokey, the whiskey he'd been drinking flavouring his mouth.

I groaned, and he yanked on the trailing rope from my wrists.

Oliver kissed down the side of my neck and sucked on my shoulder, hard enough to leave a mark, judging from the sweet sting of it.

Gabriel broke the kiss and moved back from me and Oliver let go, letting Gabriel yank me with him.

"Oliver, what do you think about tying his hands up here?" Gabriel gestured with the hand holding the rope up to the top rail of the four poster bed, over my head. "Then we can thrash him and fuck him however we want?"

I forgot how to breathe.

"Yes, that sounds rather delightful. I like the way you think." Oliver approached as Gabriel tossed the rope over the rail and tied it off, leaving me with my arms over my head and no way out.

"Oh, fuck yes," I murmured. I turned my head to watch as Gabriel smiled down at Oliver, and then, an unspoken agreement passing between then, they began to kiss. I tugged against the ropes instinctively, wanting to go to them, bask in the incredible hotness of it all.

I couldn't look away.

Gabriel, tall, gorgeous, commanding and muscular, his shirt coming off under Oliver's hands.

Oliver, surprisingly strong, buttoned down until he really wasn't... smart as a pin and willing to use his mind to get what he wanted. Now they were kissing as if it were a battle to the death and Oliver was tearing his clothes off and I was bound and watching, my cock dripping with need.

Finally they broke apart, something possibly decided between them, although whatever it was I had no idea. Had Oliver 'won' or had Gabriel? I had no idea how to gauge the result. But it didn't particularly matter, because they both closed in on me.

"Wouldn't he look nice with a collar?" Gabriel asked, in a tone that sounded idle but with an undertone of how he'd already decided what the answer should be.

"A collar? Yes, I believe I saw something in your bag?" Oliver asked. His eyes were raking my body, from my ankles to my neck, avoiding my eyes, or perhaps, for once, not being polite. Just looking at what he wanted to see.

"Indeed you did. I'll fetch it, shall I?"

I felt exposed in a way I rarely had before... and it wasn't as frightening as it probably should have been. Gabriel moved to the bag but I kept my eyes on Oliver, trying not to tremble under his gaze. Trying to be something worth the way he wanted me.

A cool piece of leather slipped around my neck, buckled tight enough so that I could feel it, but not so tight it affected my breathing. Gabriel wanted to own me, to use me, to make me his, and I wanted all of that as well. I don't know what it said about me, that I was capable of being so completely hedonistic, so willing to give up control in order to be the completed focus of Gabriel and Oliver's attention, but well, in that moment it didn't matter. I wanted to please them, I wanted to be the perfect pet, the ideal thing for them to enjoy.

"Just to confirm... What do you say if you want us to stop, Cedric?" Gabriel murmured in my ear.

"Um, I think..." I was too wrapped up in this moment I was enjoying, being the object that they both desired. Gabriel took hold of my chin and turned my face to his.

"Cedric, this is important. How do you tell us to slow down?"

I swallowed, realising he really needed me to answer. That whatever else was happening, I had to focus on this, and reassure them that I wouldn't let them break me.

"Uh, I say slow down. Or uh, stop please?" I stuttered out.

"There it is." Gabriel kissed me gently this time, reassuring me in my moment of vulnerability. I kissed him back, although I almost bit his tongue when I felt Oliver's hand on my arse, squeezing it and digging his nails into my skin. I pulled back and gasped for air as Oliver began to spank me again. Harder this time, his palm flat on my skin.

"Focus, pup." Gabriel hooked his finger into the metal ring on the front of the collar and tugged me back in for a kiss that threatened to buckle my knees.

Between Oliver's slaps and Gabriel's sensual kisses, I was soon more or less hanging from the ropes that bound me and my shoulders started to ache. The collar kept grabbing my attention, however. It certainly was a beguiling new addition that meant I didn't care at all about the ache in my muscles.

Gabriel must have taken pity on me, so he wrapped his free arm around me to help hold me up. I groaned my thanks into his mouth and bucked against him when Oliver hit me again.

Then Oliver moved away and was back with a slicked finger, teasing me open.

I moaned loudly into Gabriel's mouth and he slipped a hand down to stroke my aching cock, his movement far too slow and gentle for any kind of satisfaction.

"Ohhh, fuck please, please don't tease, I can't handle it..." I moaned. Gabriel's hand stilled and loosened and I whined.

"What did you forget?" Gabriel murmured. Oliver pushed another finger inside me. My mind scrambled to come up with an answer to his question.

Fuck, it's hard to concentrate with all these sensations... come on, what did he say at the start of all of this? Two rules. Not to speak until I was spoken to... oh yes.

"Captain. Sorry, I spoke out of turn, Captain."

"You're right, he is entirely a different person like this, isn't he?" Oliver said, fascinated.

"He loves to be bound," Gabriel said, before biting on my lower lip.

I gasped and pushed back on his fingers. I was about to beg and then remembered the first rule, so I bit my tongue instead. Gabriel stroked me quicker, with a firm hand until I was gasping, then he let go of me.

"You go first Oliver," Gabriel said. "I want to watch you with him."

"Very kind of you."

Oliver withdrew his fingers and pushed inside with his cock, filling me with his girth.

"Tell me how it feels, Cedric," Oliver ordered.

"Incredible, Sir."

Gabriel had moved a step back, and was stroking himself as he watched Oliver make me his own. He pushed deeper inside and I whined with need. My cock was utterly untouched, but I was starting to think that I could orgasm just from Oliver's cock inside me.

CHAPTER 16

IN WHICH CEDRIC IS ENJOYED BY TWO OF HIS LOVERS

The room spun a little, and I gripped the ropes with both hands, holding on for dear life.

My eyes were glued to Gabriel, watching his muscles rippling as he pumped himself, his eyes blazing, taking in me and Oliver together.

Oliver's arm locked around my waist and his mouth found my shoulder, kissing and then sucking so it stung. Leaving a mark...

I gasped and tried to push back on him, encouraging him to fuck me harder, quicker, but I couldn't say anything with my mouth about this. Words evaporated and I could only communicate with my body.

"You like that?" Gabriel growled.

My mouth dropped open and I raked him with my eyes, pleading. I nodded, since that seemed to be a way to respond.

He moved closer again, stopped touching himself and instead raked his fingernails down my chest, making me whimper with desire.

Oliver shoved his hips hard against my ass and I groaned louder still.

Gabriel closed his hand around the base of my cock and squeezed. I was throbbing and shivering and needy.

"Please, Captain…" I gasped between breaths. "Please."

"Not yet, puppy. Let your Mister Stanhope get his gratification and then it's my turn. If you keep being a good boy, then you can as well."

"Patience," Oliver grunted, as he increased his speed, getting close. "Was never something Cedric was good at."

That statement incensed me enough that I sputtered. "Rude! I waited for you for years."

Oliver's cock shoved deep inside, all the way, as he came.

"Be good, pup," Gabriel tutted and squeezed a little harder, his fingers circling my balls as well.

Oliver kissed the back of my neck and withdrew without warning. I could feel his spending dripping out of me and it made me feel like a toy, like something they were playing with. It was intoxicating.

Gabriel nodded as Oliver stroked my back and then came around to kiss the Captain.

I whimpered. Gabriel's hand was still tight around my cock and balls, and I could feel the heat of their bodies radiating towards mine. I felt my skin prickling with goosebumps.

Gabriel reached up to unloop the ropes from the bed rail and finally let go of my cock. I thought I might come on the spot, but the terror of what Gabriel would do if I orgasmed without permission stopped me, held it back.

What would he do? He'd probably tie me to a cannon and give me twenty lashes in front of the whole crew.

And I'd probably love that.

But no. I could be good tonight, for these two. I could behave.

Gabriel tugged me by my bound hands and arranged me on the bed, on my back, my hands on my chest.

"Come on, join in Oliver," Gabriel said, gesturing him

forward. Oliver climbed up on the bed beside me and started to caress my shoulders and down my sides.

Gabriel spread my legs wide and pressed gently at my hole, still slick from Oliver. He rocked his hips, teasing until I was begging him, mindless and babbling.

"Please, Captain, please please please... Put it in me, please."

Oliver leaned in to nuzzle at my neck, lipping at my earlobe as Gabriel pressed inside. He was larger than Oliver, and although I was well stretched out I felt myself adjusting around him.

"Asked so nicely," Gabriel said. He crashed his mouth against mine, his teeth tearing my lower lip so that I tasted blood.

Pity Dante's not here to taste it... I thought, wildly.

But I couldn't concentrate on much except for Gabriel's cock inside me and Oliver's hands making everything more intense.

I began to beg once more. "Please, Captain, please may I come? I need to so much..."

Oliver's hand stroked up my side, teasing, almost tickling. Gabriel's hand fisted in my hair and tugged it back as he took another kiss from my mouth. I gave it gladly, in that moment I'd have given these two men anything they asked for.

I felt a thankful, blessedly welcome hand close around my cock and start to pump. I hadn't opened my eyes for a while, so I had no idea whose hand it was. It didn't matter, all that mattered was that Gabriel said I could.

"Please, please, Captain... please, Sir..."

"Yes," Gabriel said, his voice forming possibly the most perfect and syllable that had ever been uttered.

I orgasmed along with the sibilant hissing of the end of the word. I felt my body tensing and arching off the bed as I cried out. "Yes! Yes! Fuck."

Distantly, I heard a chuckle from Oliver, and Gabriel thrust deep inside and filled me again.

I saw sparkles, or stars, or something as I gasped and moaned.

My throat felt raw from the begging and the groaning.

After a moment I emerged from the sparkles and stars and found myself unbound, Gabriel's arm around my waist and my head resting on Oliver's chest. One of them was stroking my hair, gently and warmly.

One of them was holding a cup of water to my lips and tipping it as I swallowed gratefully.

I blinked through the fuzzy lamplight until I saw Gabriel's face. He set the cup down and started to gently massage my arms, rubbing my aching muscles.

Oliver placed gentle kisses on my temple and then the top of my head.

It all felt so utterly divine, being the focus of both their attention. Like I was... important somehow. Someone worth taking care of.

CHAPTER 17

IN WHICH WE LEARN THE SOURCE OF THE GREEN LIGHT AND PLANS ARE DRAWN UP

*N*atalia had found it exceptionally easy to gain power over the governor of St Vincent. Naberus helped, of course. He had given her the nudge to attempt it in the first place. Probably, if left to her own devices, she'd have rented a townhouse in the town and made do. But Nab suggested aiming higher, and she had seen no reason to disagree with him.

They had been in their hotel room near the docks when he raised the idea, enjoying a post-coital glass of wine.

"Think of all you can do from there," Nab had said. His long fingers steepling before his mouth, obscuring it as he spoke. His gaze, as ever, was intriguing and hard to look away from.

"Is he married?" Natalia asked. Her first thought was one of seduction, as that was often the best way to get a man to do what she wanted, in her experience.

"Does it matter if he is?" Nab asked, mimicking her tone.

If anyone else had mocked or challenged her in that way, Natalia probably would have dug out a spell book and hexed them, but Nab... she never seemed to get irritated with him.

"I suppose it doesn't." Natalia allowed. She took a sip of wine. "And there's the matter of the boy, none of my usual spells have been able to locate him. He has shielded himself and that blasted ship of his from me."

Nab threaded his fingers together and sighed. "He's found a powerful witch, and there's little we can do about that. But the tattoo will be calling to him, the dreams will still leak through in some form or other."

Natalia pulled a face. "And there's absolutely no way to open the portal without him?"

"No, now that he has been marked, he is instrumental."

She had brought Nab with her when she went to call on the Governor, introducing him as a friend of the Harrow family, which wasn't even a lie.

The Governor's house was surely the most luxurious in the port of St Vincent and it bore a certain resemblance to the Harrow house in Casablanca, but on a smaller scale.

That night, she had moved into the grand house, and within three days, she had disposed of the Governor and begun to make arrangements in the house to suit her plans.

She and Nab celebrated their first night in charge of the house with a ritual that Nab taught her, something he said, that wasn't in any book.

"It will be a display of your powers, a grand display, one that people will see for miles around," he said, leading her up to the rooftop where he had already set up a spell circle.

"And a display such as this," Natalia said, who was feeling a thrill of excitement only slightly tempered by trepidation. "What is the purpose, aside from showing off?"

"If it needs another purpose, then let it be that it will summon nearby members of the Way to us," Nab said. "To swell our rank and prepare for the Chosen One."

.   .   .

Natalia settled into life in the villa, relying on Nab to keep visitors at bay, but not troubling herself with how he did so. Thus they were largely undisturbed as Natalia made her arrangements and studied the Book.

A week or so into her habitation there, she realised that access to the Governor's papers, his letterhead and his connections with the Navy could serve her very well indeed.

It was an evening's work to divine, with Nab's assistance, the names of Captain Lucifer's crew, for although she hadn't been able to locate Cedric or the ship herself, she knew that was where he would be.

If they couldn't find the ship by magic, she could flush them out with the careful and calculated use of the greediest who sailed the seas, the privateers and bounty hunters.

CHAPTER 18

Two days later, Marco came back to the inn as we were eating dinner and interrupted us. I was seated to Gabriel's right, with Dante on my other side. Oliver sat opposite me, mostly reading a book and slowly eating a bowl of seafood chowder. Dante was making his slow way through a bottle of red wine, and I had made short work of my own meal of roast pork and vegetables and was now enjoying a large slice of apple crumb cake.

"What is it, Marco?" Gabriel asked, looking up from his fifth pork rib. He was demolishing a large amount of food, which shouldn't have been as attractive as I was finding it, but here we were all the same.

Marco's face was pale and his eyes wide. He had a piece of parchment in his hand that he slapped down on the table. It had a crude rendering of him on it. Underneath were the words "Pirate on the Devil's Whore: Marco, reward: name your price."

"Name your price?" Oliver asked, frowning. "That's hardly standard terminology for a bounty."

"I'm aware of that," Marco said. He slumped down in the spare chair at our table. "This is bad."

"Exceptionally bad," Gabriel said, wiping his hands on a napkin and then picking up the paper. "Did you see any others?"

"You, Captain, and Dante," Marco said. "The bounty on one of the others had a price, substantially higher than it was last time I noticed."

"Is this... Royal Navy? I don't see any seals on it..." Oliver mused, peering at it. That was a curious point, it didn't appear to have anything to do with the navy. I didn't really know what that meant.

Dante downed his glass of wine and leaned in, speaking in a hushed tone. "A private posting, perhaps. Was the price you saw high enough for someone here to try it out?"

Marco shrugged and then grimaced. "I mean, probably."

"Fuck," Gabriel set the paper down again and went back to his meal. "Everyone act normal and finish up your dinner. We are going to leave, but we're not going to make a fuss. We don't want to rouse any attention from anyone who doesn't care for us."

I obligingly took another bite of cake, although what had been delicious and moist a moment before now tasted rather of nothing. I had to choke it down with a glass of water. My stomach sank deep into the soles of my shoes.

There is just no way this is a coincidence. It has to be related to the Cult somehow. This is my fault.

I looked up to see Oliver watching me, his shrewd expression revealing that he thought the same. He glanced at Gabriel, who met his gaze and gently nodded at me.

"I might go for an evening walk," Oliver said, lightly. "Cedric, would you care to join me?"

"I, uh, yes, of course. I should love to." My hand closed around the small drawstring bag I had tied to the belt loop of my trousers. It had the jar inside, and my fingers reached to check it was still there. This movement had become a regular tic of mine, it was comforting to know it was still there.

"Only, I need to pick up some of my equipment," Oliver continued. He set his soup spoon down and pushed the plate away from him. "In order to check the position of the stars and such. I'll just need to go to my room to retrieve it."

"Of course, I'd like to change my shoes," I said. We got up from the table together as if it had been choreographed, both moving in precise time with the other.

Dante, Gabriel, and Marco watched as we left, and a quick glance revealed Gabriel nodding his head ever so slightly at our actions.

Upstairs, Oliver vanished into his room and I went into the one I was sharing with Gabriel and Dante. I had indulged myself at a few of the local stores in the last day, and the paper packages of new clothes were still wrapped. It was going to look suspicious to walk through town with all of these... unless I pretended I wanted to stow them in the ship. Was anyone really going to notice me?

What if in the time since the witch's ritual some ship had come into port, swarming with the Cult of the Unknowable way?

My blood ran cold. The jar offered me protection but it didn't hide the existence of the Devil's Whore.

I picked up Dante's coat and slipped it on, smiling a little, because the sleeves were far too long and the shoulders a little wider than my own. I put my bundles under my arm and went back out into the hallway, where Oliver was just emerging from his room, his suitcase in his hand.

He saw me in Dante's coat and he raised his eyebrows, a smirk tugging at the corner of his mouth.

"Nice... coat?"

"You're not allowed to say anything except that I look dashing," I said, quickly. "I'm carrying it for Dante, and Dante will come with us to the ship so that we don't get attacked and killed."

"Fine you look dashing." Oliver's eyebrows pushed further up his forehead. "Don't tell me you're worried?"

"No, I'm not worried, I'm just being cautious because we don't know who might be wanting the..." I suddenly realised we were talking in a hallway full of doors, behind which could be any number of mercenaries or cultists.

Absolutely anyone could be listening to us right then. Bounty hunters, pirates, thieves... anyone!

I grabbed Oliver's hand with my free one and tugged him towards the stairs. "Let's just get started on this walk, shall we?"

Dante stood up when he saw us coming down the stairs.

"You're wearing my coat, sunshine," he said, amused.

I shrugged it off, although I had been enjoying how warm it was, but everyone seemed to think it was hilarious I wore it so I handed it to him. "Just bringing it to you. Won't you join Oliver and I on our evening stroll to map the stars?"

"It would be my pleasure."

"See you later, Lucifer..." I said, smiling at Gabriel and then leading the way out to the street. My heart began to race as we went out onto the road, and I swallowed a lump in my throat. There had been little fear in me just a few hours earlier, but the idea that someone was pursuing Gabriel and Dante and even Marco, it was a bad sign.

Part of me was relieved however, that no one had seen a poster with my image on it. Although the bounties posted would target the ship, at least no one outside of the Cult should be looking for me in particular.

My eyes darted around us as we walked towards the port. Oliver was making a show of talking about constellations, although I was sure that Dante knew them all already, and that whosoever might be listening wouldn't be fooled at all. It was far more likely that they were waiting to ambush us in some alley... much like Dante had done to me, a few months earlier in Kingston...

Although it was probably only a few minutes, the trip to get to the ship seemed to have taken hours. My feet felt every stone in the street. My lungs took in the cooling night air and the scent of jasmine, which almost smelled sickly.

I could hear my heartbeat in my ears, and my fingers felt oddly tingly where I was clutching my packages from the clothing stores.

Dante seemed to sense my distress, as he took my free arm in his. He didn't say anything at all but his presence beside me was comforting.

Or perhaps he can simply hear how loudly my blood is traversing my body and it's making him hungry.

I glanced behind me at Oliver, who gave me a bland smile back. Behind him there were two people lurking at the corner. I tightened my grip on Dante's arm, and then the two people started to kiss and I realised they hadn't been lurking at all. They'd been flirting.

Feeling ridiculous, I faced forward again. Now I was noticing every single person on the streets of Tortuga, which were busy, rowdy even.

Finally, we got to the marina where the Devil's Whore was moored. Marco was ushering a few of the crew onto the ship - he must've gone to the port inn and alerted everyone.

"You go first, Dante," I said.

"Don't be ridiculous, after you and Oliver."

I wanted to fight him on this, because he was the one with the bounty on his head, but I didn't want to make a fuss and draw attention to us.

So, I hurried up the gangplank, said good evening to Bilal, and then waited impatiently in Oliver's room with him, until Gabriel, Marco and the others were all back on board and we cast off.

CHAPTER 19

IN WHICH LIFE ON THE SHIP IS RELAXED AND PLEASANT

I slept that night with Gabriel and Dante, and I slept so well that I woke up utterly refreshed. The fears of the night before seemed totally silly, I had utterly overreacted. I reflected on my foolishness, with my back pressed against Gabriel's chest, his arm protectively wrapped around me, and my leg draped over Dante's where he lay reading in the early morning night. I couldn't remember any dreams, which was a total relief, and I didn't feel weary at all.

Dante glanced over as I stirred and gave me a soft, just-for-me smile, all indulgence and affection and general expressions he wouldn't show in front of other people if he could help it.

I smiled back up at him and felt my heart thud happily.

"Good morning, sunshine," Dante said. The pure joy that flooded me when he said that made me stretch my legs out as far as they could go.

I wriggled a little, too, and Gabriel grumbled, let go of me and turned over, putting his back to mine. I shuffled closer to Dante and reached up to touch his chest and collarbone. "You hungry?"

Dante smiled tilted his head slightly, as if to indicate that he could eat although he wasn't starving. I moved a little closer and

Dante set down his book, curling his arm around me, so I could lean against his chest. I reached up to touch his mouth, teasing his lips with my fingers until he caught my wrist with his free hand and pulled up, pressing his lips to the underside of my forearm, down from the wrist, and I felt a shiver of anticipation.

He opened his mouth and very gently sunk his fangs into my skin, closing his eyes as he drank from me. It wasn't as intense as if we'd been fucking, and in all honesty, I'd kind of expected him to take it as an invitation to fuck, but in some ways this was even better.

It felt intimate and familiar. As I wasn't distracted by fucking, it gave me the opportunity to watch as Dante's skin turned ever so slightly warmer in hue. I could see the working of his throat as he sucked and swallowed. My fingers curled, the sensation edged on pain but didn't actually get uncomfortable. Dante hummed a soft noise of satisfaction and withdrew his fangs.

Very delicately he licked at the puncture wounds he'd left in my arm, lapping at the blood that beaded there, then with his own weird vampire magic, he healed the wounds.

I cupped his face with my hand and smiled at him, and he leaned his cheek into my palm and cuddled me closer against him.

It was a lovely way to wake up, but I soon felt absolutely ravenous, which wasn't exactly a surprise, I supposed.

Dante moved aside so I could get out of bed, and I didn't bother to wash before pulling on some clothes and going in search of food.

With a belly comfortably full of tea and coconut buns, which were apparently something the cook had learned about in Hong Kong, I set up my easel, a flip book of thin canvas papers and my box of oil paints to settle into a day of doing studies of the ship.

I started with a view over the prow with the sunlight making the sea beyond sparkle. The hard lines contrasting with the ocean waves.

I was most of the way through this study when Oliver came to sit and watch me, his journal in his hand.

"Did you see a lot of exciting new things in Tortuga?" I asked, stepping back to check my perspectives were correct.

"Many things," he said. "But actually, I was up early reading a book I got from your witch friend, Tanith."

That caught my attention, so I stuck the paint brush I'd been using behind my ear and turned to him.

"Oh? I didn't know you'd gone to visit them..."

He shrugged. "Do you mind? I didn't think it'd bother you. I wanted to find out more about curses and hexes and such."

My stomach twisted. "I don't mind." I picked up a tube of cerulean and squeezed it out onto my palette, swirling it in with a bit of grey.

Why should I mind? Oliver was free to visit whomsoever he liked. It wasn't like Tanith was my particular friend or anything. But all the same, I should have liked him to check in with me first. It was my *curse after all.*

"Do you want to know what I found out?"

"Um, not really," I said, light as I could. "The jar of things Tanith and the others made seems to be working. I slept like a baby last night."

"It's only been a handful of nights, that.. Well, it may not be enough evidence to prove that it works, Cedric."

I bit my lip and swallowed the ugly fear bubbling up and cleared my throat. "Well, I guess we'll check back in a week?"

Oliver sighed, and I knew I was back to our old pattern. The feeling from how we'd acted when we were tutor and pupil and I'd desperately wanted his attention half the time because I was besotted with him. The other half of the time I wanted him to leave me alone so I could work out my sexual frustration on anyone who said yes to me...

I swallowed. Was I being unfair? After all, Oliver had been

nothing but sweet and understanding (and hot and dominant) to me.

I turned back to him and licked my lips. "Sorry, I just, uh. The witches did an amazing job, and I'd like to assume that I'm safe for the moment."

"Do you want to tell me about the ritual?" He asked. It was like being offered an olive branch. His face was open and curious now, and I realised I hadn't told him much about it at all.

"Of course." I set down my tools and I gave him as detailed a recount of the event as I could manage.

"Fascinating," he said, shaking his head with wonder. "And you could really feel the magic happening?"

"Yes, I think so. It's sort of tingly."

Oliver gave me a smile and nodded, standing up and pocketing his notebook which he had taken some notes in about the ritual. He pointed past me at the painting, mostly finished.

"That's looking good." Then he turned and went towards his cabin.

I turned the easel around and set up a fresh canvas. Now I was looking up at the mast, something of a mistake as midday drew closer and I found myself squinting, but the brightness with the proud mast and sails below did look rather striking.

I was making good headway with the soft yellow fading into blue when Gabriel stalked past with a map in his hand.

"Hey there, Captain," I said, putting some energy into the greeting that I didn't exactly feel.

He turned to me and gave me a distracted smile. "Hi, Cedric. How're you feeling?"

"Fine," I said, feeling my smile fade. "Nothing to worry about, here. I'm good."

Gabriel moved closer and put his hand on my shoulder, squeezing it warmly. He looked over at my canvas and nodded. "Pretty. I think I prefer your portraits more, though."

"Thanks?" I said, laughing a little. The compliment was

welcome, but I felt a little insulted at the same time. "I'd like to do a naked portrait of you, if you're willing to pose that is..."

Gabriel laughed darkly. "Ill pose for you like that after Dante does. In the mean time, maybe you should do this picture again, but at night. Show how it looks against the stars."

A shudder traveled down my spine and turned my stomach over.

The stars... I could paint them, but would they stay still?

Did he suggest that just to taunt me? He knows what my nightmares are, how the stars mock me... is he making fun of...

No, that's ridiculous. Of course he wouldn't be so cruel. Not to me.

I shook my head. "Um, yes, that... sounds like a nice idea. Having two side by side, night and day. Maybe I will. I'm sure Dante would like to keep me company at night..."

Gabriel pulled me in against him and kissed the top of my head. "Keep it up, puppy."

He walked away, and I felt like the stars were watching, even in the daylight. Well, they were still up there weren't they? Just the sun drowned them out.

I squinted up at the sun again and cleared my throat, trying to see only the sun.

The stars couldn't touch me now, I had my jar. The witches work and their tokens would keep me safe from them.

Wouldn't they?

CHAPTER 20

*I*t was mid morning, two days later, when the alarm bell sounded, interrupting dinner. Gabriel had organised a proper sit down dinner for once. I had suggested it was because he missed the Pickled Oyster and sitting and talking with us all, and he grunted but didn't disagree.

The wooden table in the galley that Cook usually made use of for food preparation was cleaned off and set with napkins and cutlery and everything. Dante, Oliver, and myself were all invited to join Gabriel in the meal.

We were tucking into the steamed vegetables and curried fish when the bell rang and everyone tensed. Gabriel set his fork down and stood up.

"I'd better go see what that's about, the rest of you keep eating for the moment."

He left and in a few moments, Kaito appeared at the door of the galley and caught Dante's eye. "Ship attacking, you're needed."

Dante dabbed at his mouth with his napkin before he rose gracefully. "Cedric, it's safest if you stay out of sight. This could be another ship of cultists."

Kaito hurried away as I sputtered my indignation.

"I could fight!"

Oliver shook his head and stood up as well. "Dante's right, if this is the cult they might all mob you, or just snatch you away while the rest of us fight them."

"You're going to fight, too?" I was torn between pouting and being outraged and I didn't know which emotion would allow me to get my way. I probably should have known that neither of them would.

"Yes, of course," Oliver said. "I've been practising with Gabriel in the evenings. Sword drills."

"You *have?*" I wondered how I had possibly missed this. Two of my favourite men, doing exercises with swords? In the evening? What the hell had I been doing? I should have been watching every second of that!

By the time I'd processed this thought, Dante had gone and Oliver was giving me a very severe look. I knew what he meant.

"Fine, okay, I'll just... wait in your cabin, I suppose. And hope that you can all fight off whoever it is without getting hurt..."

"That's a good boy," Oliver said. I got up to go to his cabin and he lingered long enough to give me a quick kiss on the cheek before he was jogging up to the deck. I made my way to his cabin and shut the door behind me.

Probably I should feel condescended to, him calling me a good boy, I thought. *But I actually rather liked it.*

There was nothing much to do but wait. I mean, I could have read one of his numerous books, but I wasn't in the mood for study. I took out the witches' jar and examined the contents of it.

It wasn't easy to see the wooden token in with the thick, gummy potions, herbs, ashes and crystals but he was in there. The jar felt good in my hand, comfortable and a little warm. As if I could feel the protective magic inside it.

Settling on Oliver's bed, I tucked my feet up under me and

tried not to imagine what could be happening out there without me.

It couldn't be the cult, could it? My jar was meant to help hide me, wasn't it? It was protecting my dreams and hiding me from their eyes. That's what I understood Tanith had promised.

But it was magic, and magic wasn't always reliable, was it?

Maybe I ought to just go out and sneak a look, see who's there. Who it is.

Just so that I know.

But I bit my lip and stayed put.

CHAPTER 21

IN WHICH REVELS ARE HAD

*T*he cannons had roared their last a while back, and the cabin hadn't flooded with either water or cultists, so I assumed things had turned out in our favour. It wasn't a surprise, I knew how good the crew of the Whore were in battles.

The door to the cabin opened and Oliver let himself in. He was fetchingly disheveled, his cheeks flushed with exertion and his shirt sleeves pushed up his arms. He looked good enough to bite, but I was too annoyed at being hidden away like a helpless child.

"We won, then?" I asked dryly.

He nodded, puffed out a big breath and reached his hand out towards me. "Come on, we're having a little celebration for repelling them."

I took his hand, because annoyed or not, I couldn't resist when he reached for me. His hand was hot and slightly sweaty, which just made him all the more sexy.

"Was it cultists?" I blurted. I hoped very hard that my jar had done what it was meant to do.

"I don't think so," Oliver said. "They looked like pirates to me."

"Oh you'd know," I said. "The cultists are all like, hooded and robed and like to chant my name and be all creepy and relentless."

Oliver glanced over his shoulder at me with a look of polite horror and shuddered. "No, all right, it wasn't them."

I smiled to myself, pleased that the jar had apparently worked.

Out on the deck someone had rolled out a barrel of wine, and it was flowing. Aside from the smell of gunpowder in the air and a splash of blood here and there, you almost couldn't tell that there had been a battle. There was another ship there, though, and I could see a few of the Whore's crew unloading boxes from that one onto our deck.

Gabriel looked over when Oliver tugged me up on deck and he raised a hand in greeting.

I wanted to go to him on some level, but more of me wanted to punish him a little, and I turned away, looking towards the barrel.

"I'm going to get some wine, I think." I let go of Oliver's hand and went to nudge Marco who was hanging around the spout of the barrel.

"Cup for me?" I asked, giving him a smile I didn't particularly feel.

"Of course, Ced." He offered me a cup full to the brim with red wine, Spanish if what was written on the side of the barrel was accurate. I downed half of it in one swallow and clapped him on the shoulder.

"Thank you, my good man."

Marco grinned and wrapped his arm around my shoulder, friendly and affectionate like the otter he truly was, but I just wasn't feeling it in that moment. After a few seconds I slipped out of his grip and refilled my cup.

. . .

"Come on, sunshine, don't pout," Dante murmured in my ear from behind. His arm slipped around my waist and I swallowed the urge to just melt back against him.

"I'm not pouting," I lied. "I'm righteously indignant because no one trusts me to fight and I have to be locked away like a... I don't know, like a delicate child."

Dante's breath heated my skin and his lips closed on the shell of my ear. "You're pretty delicate..."

My body responded to his closeness and the softness of his touch but delicate wasn't exactly the compliment I wanted. I huffed audibly and slowly pulled away from him.

"I'm not delicate!" It came out a little louder than I intended, and there was a momentary hush over the deck. Then a couple of sniggers and laughter.

"No, you're just in high demand," Dante said. His hand trailed down my back and I shivered again.

Gabriel had looked over when I exclaimed. He was lounging against a couple of the boxes from the other ship, one leg hitched up, and his shirt most of the way unbuttoned. He looked like the painted cover of some salacious novel.

Oliver was leaning against the mast beside him, it was clear that they'd just been talking. Although Oliver was looking over at me, slightly concerned, perhaps.

But they were getting nice and cosy with each other. I didn't know why that irritated me but it did.

I turned back to Dante, suddenly, inexplicably, close to tears. I was so... so angry and frustrated and I wanted *something*, I just didn't know what it was.

"Here," Dante said. "Have another drink." He pressed another full cup of wine into my hand.

I wasn't entirely sure that the wine was the thing I wanted, but it certainly wouldn't hurt. I took a generous gulp of wine, exhaling as it started to take the edge out of my annoyance.

Dante took my elbow and guided me towards Gabriel, who

reached out with one hand.

Fuck, I'm weak.

I took his hand and let him draw me in and kiss me. Well, I kissed him back of course. There's nothing like Gabriel's kisses. I melted against him and someone took the half cup of wine off me so I could touch his chest as we kissed.

When he was done with the kiss he pulled back and I turned to lean against him, my pout now mostly for show. I wanted attention, and now I had Gabriel, Dante and Oliver all watching me. I felt some way placated, and tried hard to forget my anger.

"So?" I said, taking my wine back from Oliver and sipping from it. "Whose ship is that?"

"Bounty hunter," Dante said.

"Must be wanted posters with that new high price everywhere," Gabriel grumbled. "But no matter, the ship is ours to sell at the next port and they had a couple of useful things aboard."

"You're not going to keep the ship and start a fleet?" I asked, nudging Gabriel with my elbow.

"No." He chuckled and gave me a wink.

"Consider it for a moment, if you had a whole fleet then you could be Commodore Lucifer."

"It does have a certain ring to it, I suppose." He tapped his fingers on my shoulder and then shook his head. "No, I think it's too much work. We'll sell her at the nearest port."

I was gazing at the ship, a little larger than the Whore, and not nearly as well cared for.

"Hey, what's... heads up!" Bilal cried, their voice carrying over the amiable noise of the crew.

"Attack!" someone else shouted, and Gabriel pulled me closer into his side, drawing his cutlass with the other hand.

"What?" Dante said, under his breath. There were no sails nearby, the bounty hunter ship had been routed... who could possibly be attacking us?

CHAPTER 22

IN WHICH ANOTHER BOUNTY HUNTER TRIES THEIR LUCK

The crew of the Whore appeared as confused as I was. Men were looking around, turning on the spot, searching the horizon for sails that weren't there.

Then there was a loud thump of a body hitting the deck and I caught sight of the attacker. He stood over Pilcher, who seemed to have been knocked down.

A huge man. Or, well. Not a man. A huge person of clearly magical descent, because their skin was the most beautiful shade of teal, with a strangely iridescent sheen over it. Their hair was long and silvery grey, and tied back in a low ponytail. They wore very little, a short skirt of fabric tied over their hips that showed off a generous amount of muscular thigh. They had a sort of bandolier or harness over their chest that was stocked with knives.

"Is that one of the merfolk?" Oliver asked, his voice full of wonder.

"Indeed it is," Gabriel said. "Block your ears lads, if they start singing we're all fucked. I'll go and see what he wants."

As if we were all carrying things around to block our ears with.

Gabriel let go of me and I went to follow him, eager to help. Oliver grabbed my arm and pulled me behind him.

"Cedric, stay back."

Dante glanced at me, obviously saw Oliver had me well in hand, and then started following Gabriel.

Oliver had drawn his sword, but done nothing about his ears. Instead he was watching with rapt attention, his eyes gleaming behind his glasses.

I wondered if Oliver would pose for me like this, with his sword in hand and looking all fearsome. I tore my eyes from him and over to the merfolk, who was also an interesting potential subject for a painting. Such fascinating colours...

"Who are you and what are you doing on my ship?" Gabriel demanded, his voice impressively loud and deep.

The merfolk straightened their back and twirled a short, slender blade that appeared to be made of some sort of stone. They hardly looked like they were about to burst into song. The closest of the crew to them was Marco, who was crouching a little, about to pounce.

"My name is Scratch, and I'm here to collect the bounty on you, Captain," the merfolk, Scratch, said. I would have thought merfolk would have better, more intriguing names than that. Perhaps it was just the name they used when they were on the surface being a bounty hunter.

"I can't believe it's really one of the merfolk, this is so fascinating, don't you think?" Oliver asked.

"Oliver, they're here to kidnap the Captain," I said.

Marco jumped at the merfolk, all coiled energy and a blade flashing in his hand. The merfolk twisted at the waist and slammed their elbow into Marco's face, dropping him to the deck with another thump.

"You're one against the whole crew," Gabriel said. "If you value your life, you'll give up and go back to where you came from."

Scratch smiled wickedly, no concern at all showing. "I'm taking you in, and collecting that reward," they said.

Gabriel brought his sword into guard position.

Dante was at his side, his shoulders hunched. The merfolk opened their mouth and a sound came out.

I slammed my palms over Oliver's ears without particularly thinking about it. He seemed to have no sense of self preservation at all.

Of course, now I can hear what the song sounds like...

The song was beautiful, absolutely eerie and haunting. As soon as I heard it, I felt a sort of ease wash over me, the same kind of soothing feeling that getting drunk gave me. I watched as Gabriel seemed to falter, his cutlass tip drooping towards the deck. I saw it but I didn't feel worried or upset for Gabriel.

Scratch's expression was one of confident amusement. They knew they'd already won. All around me the crew of the Whore were relaxing, putting their weapons down, stepping back.

There was an itching on my back but I felt it distantly. I wondered why I was holding onto Oliver's ears, and started to remove my hands, but he gripped my wrists and kept them in place.

"Don't let go, Cedric. I might still be able to help."

His words didn't make a lot of sense, but I liked the way his hands felt on my wrists so I didn't move.

Scratch's song continued, and they moved closer to Gabriel. My heart thumped, and I felt a sudden flash of pain from my back. My tattoo... what was my tattoo doing?

My head cleared a little. I became aware of the danger we were all in.

Perhaps the pain had cleared my head? Had my tattoo flared with pain to protect me?

Scratch took another step towards Gabriel and I cried out. "No!"

This seemed to have an effect on Dante, who suddenly

sprang forward, tackling Scratch to the deck. The two of them wrestled, rolling over each other. Scratch's song cut off suddenly and Gabriel seemed to shake himself and raise his cutlass.

Dante and Scratch were locked together, both of them growling and spitting as they struggled. Bilal had to leap out of the way as they rolled against a barrel. Dante hissed and reared up, showing his long fangs, before sinking them into the merfolk's shoulder.

Scratch hissed and went limp, their blade fell from their hand. Gabriel stalked closer and stood over the two of them.

"Don't kill them," Gabriel said.

Oliver's grip loosened and I let go of his ears. As soon as I let go, he was striding across the deck to join Gabriel. I followed a little further behind.

Dante sat up, one hand still on Scratch's shoulder. "They'll be somewhat subdued for a while, merfolk are particularly susceptible to vampire venom."

"Venom?" Oliver exclaimed. "You have *venom?*"

"Not the time, Oliver," Gabriel said. Oliver twisted his hands together and bit his lip, for once the one being told off.

I moved a couple of steps closer.

"You don't want them killed? Shall I take them to a cell?" Dante asked.

"Please, I'll check on the others."

I'd all but forgotten that Pilcher and Marco had been hurt. I watched as Dante pulled Scratch's arm around his neck, and then hauled their body up on his back. I knew he had vampire strength but it was still interesting to watch. Oliver was also watching closely, I could practically see him making notes. Then he seemed to shake himself and went to help Gabriel with Marco.

Kaito had brought a small silver vial out of his pocket and was waving it under Pilcher's nose. He came to with a start, swearing.

Marco was half sitting up, one hand over his nose, looking rather put out. His nose must have been gushing blood as it soaked his chin, throat and shirt. Oliver pinched the bridge of his nose. "Just let me keep the pressure on it, it should stop in a moment."

Gabriel, straightened up, apparently leaving Marco's treatment to Oliver.

They must have really bonded. There's respect there now between them.

Gabriel cleared his throat and addressed the crew.

"It seems Scratch was working alone, but just to be on the safe side, up anchor and let's get a few leagues from here."

CHAPTER 23

*K*aito and Oliver helped Pilcher and Marco below
deck and I followed, because Gabriel was at the
helm, and Dante hadn't yet emerged from the brig. Part of me
wanted to follow Oliver, just because it was him, but I also
wanted to sneak a look at Scratch if possible.

I'd never seen a member of the merfolk before, that I knew
of, let alone been threatened by one. Well, I guessed they hadn't
exactly threatened *me*, but they'd definitely threatened the ship
as a whole by targeting Gabriel. It was all rather exciting.

But first we had to ensure Marco and Pilcher were all right,
naturally. I helped Oliver by staying out of the way and lingering
near the door, listening for Dante's voice.

Oliver seemed to know rather a lot about first aid, because
he was pressing and prodding at Marco's neck for a while before
declaring him sound.

"It still hurts," Marco grumbled.

Kaito passed him a glass bottle and Marco swigged from it.

"Ooh, is that rum? Can I've a little?" I asked.

"It's medicinal," Oliver said. "And no you can't."

"Spoilsport."

Pilcher was declared in need of bedrest, but also to not fall asleep, so Marco volunteered to stay with him in the small cabin for the next few hours.

"If he falls asleep he may not wake up again," Oliver said. "So, keep him distracted, but make sure he rests. And drinks plenty of water."

"Aye," Marco said. He settled in the chair beside the cot and Kaito, Oliver and I left them to it.

Oliver grasped my elbow, which was a very welcome action indeed. I felt myself perk up all over, suddenly imagining he was going to guide me to his room, undress me and explore every inch of my body with his tongue.

"Oliver," I said, letting my voice drop to low and seductive, leaning in towards him. "Is there something you'd like?"

"I want to see the merperson," Oliver replied. His hand tightened on my elbow. "Where's the brig?"

Oh. I tried not to be visibly disappointed.

"Uh, below I think. When they kidnapped me they just used your room as a cell and locked it from the outside. Well, it wasn't your room then. And it was very bare. But it was... where they kept me. I guess if there's a proper brig it'd be further down?"

Oliver nodded and started towards the access ladder to the lowest deck. I followed, curious as well.

The lowest deck did indeed house a proper brig, with iron bars and shackles. I wondered briefly why Gabriel hadn't stashed me down here when they'd brought me aboard as a hostage. Perhaps because they didn't see me as a threat... or even particularly dangerous. Which, well, it was largely a fair assumption.

In the brig, the merfolk was sitting, their back propped against the wall, they appeared to be awake, but very sick, tired out perhaps.

The bandolier of blades was now over Dante's shoulder, and he had a selection of other weapons in a small box at his feet. Dante looked to Oliver and me as we approached.

His forehead crinkled and he frowned. "What are you two doing down here?"

"We wanted to see the merfolk," I said, because I'd never been able to lie to Dante, even if it made us sound sort of childish.

"If it's all right," Oliver said. "I've never... I'd love to make some observations, perhaps send a scientific paper to Oxford or something."

I glanced at him, surprised. I mean, I knew he liked to learn and all that, but I had no idea he'd been considering writing papers.

Dante huffed a little, but stepped aside, gesturing for us to approach. "My venom will work as a natural sedative for a few hours at least."

"I still can't believe you have venom," Oliver muttered. "But we can talk about that later."

"Do you put venom in me, when you bite me?" I asked, moving close enough to Dante that I could slip an arm around his waist.

"Yes," he said, promptly. That knowledge made me feel a little uncomfortable, until he elaborated. "It dulls the worst of the pain and makes it pleasurable, but if you get too much of it in your body, and if you were to drink my blood, you'd start to turn."

I swallowed, my mouth suddenly dry. I tensed, and almost pulled away from him before stopping myself.

We'd never talked about *turning* before.

Dante picked up on my flush of fear because he shook his head quickly. "You're in no danger of that, sunshine. It's a lot of venom needed, and then the blood exchange, it's a whole ritual and... yes, you're quite safe. Merfolk's biology is sufficiently different from a... a land based human, that it works in a different way."

"Fascinating," Oliver breathed. He was close to the bars, peering in.

"What's fascinating?" Scratch asked, startling me so that I jumped against Dante and he held me even closer.

"You are," Oliver said. "Would you mind telling me about how you grew up? Could you always change forms or is it something you learned?"

Scratch blinked blearily at Oliver. "What?"

There was a noise behind us and I turned to see Gabriel descending.

"Well, what did you find out?"

"Nothing," Dante said. He kissed the top of my head and let go of me, so he could hand Gabriel the bandolier. "They've only just found their voice."

"Hm." Gabriel moved to where Oliver was and raised his voice. "Scratch, who sent you?"

"I was four cycles old when I learned how to shift," Scratch replied. Then they laughed, a delighted, and clearly inebriated sort of laugh. "My mothers thought I was very clever. I found a jellyfish that had been washed ashore and returned it to the ocean. It was a great friend…"

Gabriel folded his arms and glared. "What?"

"Oh, that's … that's because of what I asked," Oliver said. "Sorry, should we get out of your way? I'll uh, I'll come back when they're a bit more clear-headed."

"That would probably be for the best."

"What are you planning to do with them, Captain?" Dante asked. Oliver turned towards the ladder, but he was moving sort of slowly, so I moved even more slowly to follow him, both of us listening.

"Find out where they were going to take me, and if there are any other cursed merfolk waiting to attack the ship from below."

Scratch made a long, protracted farting noise with their mouth, and then giggled.

Gabriel rounded on them, if the bars hadn't been in the way, I think he would have strode over and done something intimidating with his cutlass but as it was he smacked the flat of his palm against the bars, making a noise that startled all of us.

"Who are you working with?"

"None," Scratch said. Their mirth seemed to bleed away and was replaced with sadness. "Just Scratch, s'why I changed my name. No one liked me, no one understood. The whole clan, they just..." they made the farting noise again and closed their eyes. "I'm tired."

"Will the venom affect them permanently?" Oliver asked Dante. I looked at him askance.

"Your fascination with venom is getting rather disturbing," I said.

"We can talk about that later," Dante said, softly.

Gabriel glared in at Scratch. "Did the Cult of the Unknowable Way send you?"

"Bounty was high," Scratch said, then they yawned hugely, settled on their side and went to sleep.

Dante exhaled. "The venom won't harm them, it will wear off in a few hours."

"And you're sure you got all their weapons off them?" Gabriel asked. Dante nodded. "Yes, but uh, it's merfolk, they could sing again."

There was a moment while we all looked at the slumbering merfolk and then at each other. I remembered with a start that it hadn't exactly worked on me when they'd sung before.

"I think... I think my tattoo did something when they sang, before..."

"Yes, you called out," Dante said. "Everyone else was entranced."

"Well what does *that* mean?" Gabriel exclaimed. There was a vein throbbing in his forehead and he shoved a hand through his hair, practically growling. "Fuck!"

He went to storm out, which was difficult since he had to climb the ladder. Oliver murmured something to Dante, probably asking him something about venom...

"Everyone out," Gabriel called as he scaled the wooden ladder. "I'll set guards and tell them to plug their ears, just in case."

CHAPTER 24

IN WHICH THE CREW MAKES PLANS

*T*hat night, Gabriel called a meeting in his cabin, inviting Dante, Bilal and Kaito to discuss their unusual prisoner. Gabriel stood, his arms firmly crossed. Bilal was leaning against his desk, and Kaito lounged against the wall near the door, one hand on his weapon as if he expected another attack any moment. Dante was on Gabriel's bed, apparently quite at home there, now. Gabriel set that observation aside to consider later.

"Throwing them back into the ocean doesn't seem like it would solve any of the problems," Bilal said.

"We could just kill them," Kaito said. Gabriel drummed his fingers on his biceps and scowled.

"I don't wish to kill them, something feels off about killing a mer..."

In truth, Gabriel was a little more afraid of the merfolk than he wished to let on. He could recall his mother telling him tales of their kind, of the strange rituals and the apparently endless wars they engaged in under the waves. Besides, he felt a little bad for Scratch, after they'd said about working alone and their clan apparently shunning them.

It felt uncomfortably familiar. His own background wasn't

exactly different from that, except in England instead of in the ocean.

The others didn't argue with him. Sailors were plenty superstitious and the merfolk were mysterious as a species. In fact, it wasn't clear if there were multiple species of merfolk or just the one. But there were plenty of unknowns, which meant they should probably stay away from killing the mer.

"Keeping them on board would please young Mister Stanhope," Dante said, drily.

Gabriel huffed his breath out. "I'm not concerned with providing Stanhope with scientific specimens, I want to keep our crew safe and evade these bounty hunters. And I want to keep Cedric out of the hands of that blasted cult, which I am sure are behind this somehow."

Kaito cleared his throat. "If the bounty is this high, it's going to be extraordinarily difficult. We might need to find who is posting such high rewards."

Gabriel sighed and dropped his arms to his sides, trying to shake out the tension he was holding in his shoulders and failing. He had to make a decision about this, and soon.

"There was that strange green light," Dante said. "Over Saint Vincent. Odds are that's the Cult at work. It could be related."

"We don't know it's related," Gabriel said. "But I don't particularly believe in coincidences. No private parties have posted bounty for me before, as far as I'm aware."

"The woman, Natalia Harrow, escaped us back in Casablanca," Dante said. This irritated Gabriel even further. He didn't like to be reminded of loose ends.

"If they're there, and we sail to them, we could be walking right into a trap," Bilal said.

"In the morning I'll try again with Scratch," Dante said. "Perhaps Cedric could come, he didn't seem to be enchanted and his call snapped me out of it, after all. Perhaps I can learn some more about where they learned about the bounty in the first place."

"In the meantime, we'll make course for a small island, or archipelago, and hide for a few days," Gabriel said. "On the way we'll stop at the biggest port only long enough to sell the captured ship, and Kaito will handle the sale, the rest of us stay aboard and out of sight."

Dante cleared his throat. "As to a place to hide... The uh, the Splintered Isles are nearby. People may not pursue us there."

Gabriel rolled his eyes. "Yes, because those are cursed waters and we'd probably sail right into rocks, or some vengeful sea witch."

"Perhaps we can find somewhere close enough to scare others off, but without actually entering the cursed waters?" Kaito ventured.

"Fine," Gabriel said. "Make us a route and we'll adjust our direction."

Kaito pushed off from the wall. "Is that all, Captain?"

"Yes," Gabriel replied. "No, double the guard. I don't want to be taken by surprise again, and remember to tell the crew, we need at least half of us to have blocked ears. And everyone when they go below."

On the deck, Cedric had set up his easel and a new canvas, this one had been primed with navy blue and he was making a copy of the one he'd done in the sunshine, a view up to the main mast. Or at least, that had been the plan, Gabriel understood. He couldn't see too much of the canvas, as it was behind Cedric and lit from the side. He also had a lantern hung over it so the mast was lit up somewhat.

Gabriel had a slight ache in his head, but felt too on edge to relax. He wandered over to watch.

Cedric being artistic was still amusing in some way to him,

or perhaps a better term was intriguing. Besides, it reminded him of the beautiful studies of each of the crew that he'd made before they'd handed him over to the cult in Casablanca.

Thinking of that time made his head ache more.

"Evening," Gabriel said. Cedric didn't respond. He was stroking the brush over the canvas with an intense gaze. Gabriel tried again. "Good evening, Cedric."

Cedric turned to look up from his paint palette, seemed to finally notice Gabriel, and gave him a distracted smile. "Plans made, are they?"

"More or less," Gabriel said. "We're going to hide for a bit, near the Splintered Isles."

"What are the Splintered Isles?" Cedric yawned and stretched his arms over his head. Gabriel saw a little drip of blue paint on his cheek. It was frustratingly adorable.

Gabriel felt the throb in his head ease a little and he reached out to try and wipe the paint off with his thumb. It was wet so he smudged it instead. Cedric giggled a little. "You didn't answer my question."

"The Splintered Isles are cursed waters. Lots of merfolk there, but there's other things as well, many a ship has been lost there, many crews killed. Storms and mists and all sorts of things that can't be explained," Gabriel said. "A lot of folks, including myself, are afraid to sail that channel, so it could be a safe hiding spot."

Cedric wrinkled his nose in distaste. "I feel like we have enough curses as it is, is it really necessary to go where there could be more?"

"It's the safest place for us to hide out while we determine who set these rewards on us," Gabriel said. He didn't like the queasy feeling he was getting and he wasn't exactly sure where it was coming from.

Cedric turned back to his painting, distracted, and Gabriel moved closer to see how it was progressing.

The queasy feeling resolved itself into full blown fear as he saw the image on the canvas. The ship's mast in the lantern light, stretching up to the starry sky. But there was something else up there - something lurking in the stars, something with bright glowing eyes and tentacles that reached towards the viewer.

Objectively the picture was very finely rendered.

But it revolted and frightened Gabriel on a deep level. He didn't hesitate, he pushed Cedric aside from the canvas, ignoring his cry of protest, and picked the canvas up in both hands.

"What are you doing? It's not even dry yet!"

Gabriel turned, couldn't see Dante, so called for him instead. "Quartermaster!"

Dante emerged from below deck. "Yes, Captain?"

"Cedric's just painted... I don't know what. Come on," he led the way into his cabin, where the light was better. Cedric hurried behind him, still protesting.

"Give that back, I wasn't finished. Look, what exactly is the problem?"

Gabriel didn't look at him, he set the painting on a chair and pointed at it.

"What?" Cedric spread his arms to indicate he didn't understand, and then took another look at the painting and paled.

"Yes, exactly," Gabriel said. "What were you thinking, painting the images from your nightmare?"

"I didn't..." Cedric glanced over his shoulder at Dante, who moved closer behind him, putting a hand on his waist. "I didn't intend to. I thought... I was just painting the sky."

"You were paying full attention the entire time?" Dante asked.

"Well, sometimes when I paint I kind of lose myself in it," Cedric said. He rubbed the back of his neck and looked younger all of a sudden. Lost. Gabriel hated seeing that, it made him want to fight the world so that Cedric would never look lost again.

Dante sighed. "The magic is finding another way through to you."

Cedric shuddered and stepped back, pressing himself against Dante, who put his arms around him. "The charm should keep it away, shouldn't it?"

"Apparently not," Gabriel scowled at the canvas. "Maybe we should burn it."

"I do not think the canvas itself will be dangerous," Dante said, but there wasn't enough certainty in his tone to reassure Gabriel.

"No, you can't just *burn* it!' Cedric exclaimed. "I can paint over the creepy bit! I can, uh, I have some solvent, we can just strip the paint right off it."

"Dante? Will that rid us of whatever magic has... made this happen?"

"I really don't know," Dante said, softly. Gabriel narrowed his eyes at Dante, feeling outnumbered. Dante didn't want to side with Gabriel, he didn't want Cedric angry with him. But Gabriel had to consider the ship as a whole, and all the people on it.

"What if you go to paint it again and the same thing happens, what then?"

Cedric opened his mouth, closed it again. His brow furrowed and he shook his head slightly. "I don't know."

Gabriel squared his shoulders. It was a harsh decision but he had to do it.

"I won't have this hanging about on my ship and scaring the crew, or... summoning something to us," he said. He picked up the canvas and a candle and took them out to the deck.

"Wait, Gabriel... Captain, please!" Cedric followed, protesting as he strode to the side of the ship.

Cedric lunged and took hold of Gabriel's arm, presumably to

beg him to reconsider, but Gabriel shook him off. "I'm sorry Cedric, there's no other way."

"Captain! I worked hard on that, I can... I can paint over it!"

"No, Cedric."

It was a moment's work to set it alight and then toss the burning canvas onto the ocean.

Cedric and Dante had joined him, and Cedric made a small, sad noise as they all watched the canvas burn. The noise wrenched at something deep inside Gabriel. His heart thumped and he wondered briefly if he hadn't been too harsh... but no, whatever that had been it was likely to haunt Gabriel's dreams now, even without magical intervention.

He helped Cedric pack up his paints and spare canvases, trying to atone for being harsh with his painting, but Cedric wouldn't meet his eyes.

CHAPTER 25

IN WHICH GABRIEL IS SICK OF THIS WHOLE THING

People were shouting. Why were they shouting?

I was cold... dreaming? Was I out on the deck again?

There isn't usually this smell in my dreams, is there?

A sharp, searing pain woke me up. My eyes flew open but I didn't understand what I was seeing. It wasn't the inside of the captain's cabin. It wasn't a deserted deck with stars above. It was a deck swarming with men, fighting.

One of them had just sliced into my arm. I glanced down to see the blood dripping out of my arm and soaking the fabric of my nightshirt. I looked up again, my heart in my mouth. I still couldn't understand what was going on.

The man who'd stabbed me turned to clash swords with Gabriel, who had come down on him with a terrifying war cry. Beyond them I saw Kaito choking a man with a thick rope.

Someone grabbed my arm and yanked me backwards. I lost my footing, I wasn't wearing shoes and my feet skidded on something wet on the boards. Blood. It was probably mine.

I twisted, trying to get my arm free from whoever was gripping me, trying to see who it was.

The faint hope that it was one of the crew rescuing me died as I saw my captor.

The man had a full beard, salt and peppered, and his eyes were blazing. He tugged me closer to him, his mouth splitting in a smile. "Maybe the Captain will go quietly if I bring his little slut along..."

"Fuck you." I spat in his face. Although, truly, I was the Captain's slut, that wasn't for this random stranger to say, and I certainly wasn't going to go with him willingly.

"Ah, so you *are* the Captain's slut!" He wrapped his forearm around my neck. I tried to stomp on his foot, but I couldn't get a lot of impact into it.

"Let go of me you disgusting oaf!"

That seemed to get someone's attention, because the man made a surprised noise. "Urgh."

His arm went loose and I pulled out of his grip, shuddering and turning to see what had happened.

Dante had run him through with a long knife I'd not seen before. "Cedric, what are you doing out here?" He reached for me and I took his hand, knowing whatever was going on, I'd be safer if I was close to him. Dante looked pointedly at the bleeding wound on my arm and then back into my eyes. I clasped my free hand over it to staunch the bleeding a little.

"I have no idea, honestly. What's going on?"

"Another bounty hunter," he said. He drew me behind him, positioning me between him and the edge of the ship and shielding me with his body. I peered over his shoulder and saw Gabriel slit a man's throat, dressed in black trousers and little else. Blood had spattered over his chest and neck. Around him the battle seemed to ease. Dead bodies littered the ship and I could see a small ship just off the other side of the Whore.

How had this happened? How had I slept through the alarm bell, which would certainly have rung, wouldn't it?

And how was I out here on the deck in the middle of a fight?

How did any of this happen?

"Clear the deck," Gabriel said, wearily. It was the dead of

night, close to dawn I thought. The enemy must have meant to attack while most of the crew slept.

Bilal hopped past, Marco supporting them, they seemed to have some kind of leg injury. They went below deck, presumably to get Bilal some medical attention.

I breathed out heavily, trying to make sense of it. I looked up to see the stars, which were largely visible, a small cloud here and there but most of them twinkling down. They weren't moving, which was a saving grace I had barely allowed myself to hope for.

Dante turned back to me. "Cedric, what were you doing out here?"

I shrugged, wincing as the movement made the wound in my arm throb with pain. Dante's attention switched to my blood again and I swallowed. "I have no idea, I thought I was dreaming."

Kaito tipped a body overboard beside us and then approached, looking at me with a frown. "Are you all right?"

"I got sliced," I said.

"I think you were sleepwalking," he said.

"Sleepwalking? I've never sleepwalked in my life."

"How about we take care of that wound and then we talk about what happened," Dante said, his voice urgent.

"Right, yes," I said. "Great, I'd like that. Yes."

"Were you having the dream again?" Dante asked as he escorted me back to the Captain's cabin. His voice was low, tense, as if he was frightened of how I would answer. I thought as hard as I could but there was just... nothingness, until I'd started to wake up.

"No, no dreams. Although when I felt the boards under my feet I thought I was back in the dream. It was just blackness, a void, I guess."

I frowned, uncertain as to why I'd used the word void. It felt dangerous somehow, like I was poking at the edge of something I shouldn't be.

Best not to think too hard about that.

"But you were still drawn into the middle of a fight... you could have been hurt or killed."

I swallowed. "I don't know what happened," I said. My arm throbbed. "And I'm in rather a lot of pain..."

In half an hour, Dante had cleaned up my arm, with a surprising lack of licking, and rather more damp cloth and bandaging than I'd expected. "I thought you were going to, you know, take advantage," I said, giving him a seductive smile.

Dante pursed his lips and shook his head. "It's not the time, regardless of how delicious your blood smells. I'm too concerned about you."

"Aw, I knew you cared about me."

"I've told you that I care about you." He lifted my hand to his lips and kissed the back of it gently. My heart fluttered at the sensation and I felt my cheeks flush.

This was better, flirting and being a general annoyance, it kept the confusion and fear away.

Gabriel slammed the cabin door open and stalked in. Oliver followed close behind, moving at a run.

"What the Hell just happened, did I see Cedric up on the deck?" Oliver demanded, he skidded to a stop beside the bed and looked me over. His glasses were smudged with grime, his hair was in disarray, and he looked devastatingly handsome. "Are you all right?"

"Yes, I'm fine," I said, a little pleased that he'd been so worried. But also mostly afraid because it was alarming that I'd wandered out there. I tried to make a joke out of it, and lighten the mood. "Not as stabbed as I was in Casablanca."

"How can you joke about being stabbed?" Oliver raked his hands through his hair.

"It was another bounty hunter, how are they all finding us is what I want to know," Gabriel said. He frowned at me, then moved closer to check how Dante had cared for my arm.

"They thought you'd go with them if they stole me," I said, as I remembered. "They really wanted you, Gabriel."

He paced the room, his shoulders tense and his entire being filling the room with annoyance. "We'll get to the Splintered Isles tomorrow, hide out between the islands or something and think of a better plan," he said, finally. "For now we need to lick our wounds and regroup."

I saw an opportunity to lighten the mood again.

"Dante loves to lick wounds!"

Dante covered his eyes with his hand and sighed, long sufferingly. I grinned at Gabriel but he shook his head and Oliver patted my shoulder in a sort of placating way.

"Maybe you should just go back to sleep, Cedric?"

CHAPTER 26

IN WHICH BORED SHIPMATES MAKE
SOME FUN

*I*n the hours it took us to sail to the Splintered isles. I sat with Marco and Bilal near the prow of the ship and took in some sun.

Marco told me the tales he'd heard of ships being wrecked on the sharp rocks, and the vicious merfolk who lived in the area and swarmed ships just to eat the sailor's flesh.

Bilal, who was on rest with a sprained ankle from the battle, their leg bandaged to a splint, and cranky with the pain of it, told stories of strange voices on the wind that lured ships into the sharp rocks on purpose.

"That's the same as my story," Marco said.

"No, yours was just bad sailors hitting the rocks," Bilal said. "Mine is about people being intentionally lured into the rocks."

Marco rolled his eyes. "Barely a difference."

"Fine, I've also heard of an unnatural fog that stirs up out of nowhere, becalming ships so they can't escape as sirens and witches swarm them and eat their souls," Bilal said, rather more forcefully.

"Sounds... frightening?" I ventured.

"The point is that there's weird magic and monsters there."

"Monsters like the one in the brig?" I asked. Scratch hadn't been released, since no one could come up with a compelling reason for them not to just immediately attack again if we let them go. Unless we paid them more than the bounty on Gabriel's head, but the ship wasn't carrying that much treasure and even if it was, Gabriel wouldn't give it up so easily.

"Exactly," Bilal said. "And fey folk…" they eyed Marco slightly suspiciously. "Like you?"

"I'm not fey," Marco said, his eyebrows drawing together. "I'm just an otter."

"Not all otters can change forms. There's definitely magic involved somewhere."

"My raft has just always been able to," he shrugged.

"Your… I'm sorry, it sounded like you said your raft," I said. "Must've misheard you."

"You didn't, that's what we call ourselves. Like, the pirates are a crew, my otter family is a raft." He grinned at me as if it made any kind of sense.

I nodded. "Right, yes, silly of me…"

Bilal snorted. "I don't see how otters can just spontaneously learn how to turn into humans, there's got to be fey or witch influence in there somewhere."

"I don't know, maybe there was, but it wasn't in my lifetime or my parent's, or they'd have told me about it."

"Hmm, well, maybe you should look into it, maybe you have magic powers that you've never used."

Marco shrugged, leaned back on his hands and turned his face up to the sun. "Don't care. I'm happy as I am."

I bit my lip, feeling envious even though I didn't particularly covet anything Marco had. I imagined turning into an otter and swimming in the ocean would be fun, but I didn't want to do it really. He didn't have a lover, or much at all beyond a couple of changes of clothes… but he was so happy in his skin. So content with his lot.

Am I not content?

Well, no, of course I'm not, I'm plagued with nightmares and there's a cursed tattoo on my back. And that weird thing happened with something... unnatural appeared on my painting that I didn't paint. And the sleepwalking into a sword fight.

I looked over at the rest of the crew, my eyes inevitably landing on Gabriel at the helm. He had questioned me about the sleepwalking as well, until I'd felt utterly hopeless, not having any kind of answer that could please him.

How could I possibly get rid of the tattoo and lose the interest of the cult? Surely it was my fault that Gabriel was so hotly pursued. The idea that I was putting the ship in danger made me feel physically sick.

Maybe I ought to just hand myself over to the cult, it would take the attention off the Devil's Whore and the souls upon it.

I wondered if Dante or Oliver, or even Gabriel would let me turn myself over.

Not that I wanted to. From what I knew of the cult it wouldn't simply be a ritual they wanted to do with me and my tattoo.

If they had their way, the cult would kill me and use the tattoo to bring unholy horrors from beyond the veil down on this world.

So, actually, if I were to give myself up to save the crew, it wouldn't be a sacrifice of any noble kind, it would be me ensuring mass destruction and death.

The crew of the Devil's Whore would surely die when those things came from beyond the stars.

It simply wasn't an option.

I had no options as far as I could see.

We arrived in the archipelago that made up the Splintered Isles shortly after midday, and I had to say, it wasn't nearly as threatening or frightening as Bilal and Marco had made it sound.

The Devil's Whore slowly navigated its way into the sheltered cove of a densely wooded island and dropped anchor. The sails were furled and secured, and the crew set about cleaning the deck, washing clothes, and chores like that.

I had an itch that wouldn't leave me alone. My mind kept on spiralling back to the 'I have no options' place, and I didn't like it one bit. I wanted distraction. Something to stop me fixating on my tattoo, that painting and the sleepwalking.

Gabriel's mood hadn't lifted at all, and Oliver was down in the brig talking to Scratch, or trying to, so I sought out Dante to see what he was doing.

Dante was in his cabin, writing in a book. He looked up when I knocked on his open door and set his quill aside, blowing on the ink to dry it off.

"What are you doing?" I ambled into the room, sticking my hands in my pockets and trying to look delicious. It wasn't exactly something I knew how to project, but it had to do with the buttons I'd undone on my shirt and pushing my shoulders down and back to show off my throat.

"I was updating the log of supplies," Dante said. "But now I think I'm about to be distracted."

A smile played around Dante's lips and I felt like I'd won something. He wasn't going to ignore me or blow me off. I didn't have to think too hard about anything but him.

Dante closed the book, smiled indulgently and leaned back in his chair.

I pulled my hand out of my pockets and stroked through his hair, pushing it back behind his ear.

"You are correct."

His hand moved around my waist, tugging me gently closer, so I climbed into his lap, my legs straddling his hips. I wiggled my hips, in the guise of getting more comfortable and was rewarded with a soft moan.

"You are insatiable," he said.

147

"Not the first time I've been told that," I said. "On the chair or the bed?"

"So very charming," Dante said, his voice dripping with sarcasm. "But bed. I think I've been sitting here long enough."

"Then you'd better get us over there." I twined my arms around his neck. "Show me that extraordinary vampiric strength I know you possess."

"Is that an order?" Dante raised one perfect eyebrow and I felt a thrill of excitement and even more arousal.

"Oh, definitely."

If there was one thing I knew about Dante, aside from his being a vampire, it was that he held himself back a lot. He was meticulously careful with his hunger, and I'd never seen him lose control - well, he'd almost lost control the first time we kissed, but I expect that was the sheer surprise of how much I wanted him. Or something.

But control was the key word. Dante had so much of it, every day, in every part of his life. I'd seen a little from our encounters in Gabriel's cabin together, that he liked the idea of submission. In a way it made perfect sense to me, he was giving up his control to another, and in that moment he could be exactly himself.

The trick was to get him to let his guard down in the first place, and apparently I had already managed that. I just had to pursue it.

Dante slipped a hand under my arse, stood up and carried me to the bed one handed. I was holding onto his neck, but I could tell I barely needed to.

It was fucking hot.

My breath came quickly as he dumped me unceremoniously on the bed. I laughed despite myself, and then thought I ought to be a bit more commanding. I went to my knees and beckoned Dante closer. He sank onto the bed, facing me on his knees. I started to undo his shirt.

"Are you hungry?"

Dante's throat worked as he swallowed hard. "Yes."

"Then you'll do as I say. You may undress yourself and then me." I dropped my hands to my sides and he shrugged out of his shirt, then went to undo his trousers.

As I had suspected, he relished the thought of relinquishing control as much as I did with Gabriel.

He made quick work of stripping the both of us, and then I pushed him onto his back and climbed on top of him. Kneeling so that I was pinning his legs with mine, I pressed my forearm on his chest, leaned in and kissed him hard. His hands found my waist, and caressed the curve there, before sliding down to squeeze my arse. It felt incredible, his cool hands on my hot skin.

I can't believe I get to do this, I thought, giddy with it. *He's so strong and magical, and he'll let me have my way with him.*

My cock was throbbing with need and I rocked my hips, rubbing my cock against Dante's until both of us were moaning.

"Please," he gasped in between moans. "Fuck me or ride me or something, I can't stand the teasing..."

Well, isn't that interesting to know...?

I reached into the drawer beside his bed and pulled out the pot of coconut oil I knew would be there. *Hmmm... wouldn't it be fun if I could bind him, too?*

"I don't suppose you have any rope in here?" I asked. Although as I asked it I felt sure the answer would be yes, since he had so expertly tied me up in the past.

"Bottom drawer," Dante said, his voice strangled. His expression was a kind of rapt nervousness.

"May I use it to tie you up? I was thinking of your hands, so that you can't touch me."

Dante breathed out, ragged and laden with need, and he nodded. "Y-Yes, you may. I'd... quite like that," he said. It was a weirdly formal response and I smirked, but let go of him to lean over and down to the bottom drawer, where there was a coiled hank of rope that was silky to the to touch, pale cream in colour.

"Oooh, this is lovely," I said, pulling it into my hands.

"Asanawa," Dante said. "From Japan, many... many years ago I spent some time in Tokyo, there are places you can go... they have an incredible practice of bondage there."

"You'll have to forgive me for using it in a rather basic manner then," I said. "And you must promise to take me to Tokyo and show me this incredible bondage."

"I'd love that, if you don't mind a long voyage."

"I'm sure you could keep me amused." I smiled and kissed him gently before sitting up and getting to work.

I began wrapping the rope around his wrists, making several loops before wrapping it around the rope between his wrists. He continued to talk, offering no resistance as I took away a little more of his control. I knotted it tight and tugged on it to ensure it was secure. "They call it shibari, or kinbaku, the art of beautiful bondage. Sometimes they will suspend someone just by the ropes on their body. The shapes and forms they can make..."

His eyes fluttered shut as he remembered. I looped the ends of the rope up and over the rail at the head of Dante's bed and knotted it there, his arms stretched over his head.

I sat back, taking it all in and imagining what an incredible erotic portrait it would make... *if I could paint it without some magical interference that is.*

I dismissed that thought and moved down his body, planting kisses here and there on his chest and torso.

He moaned so softly I almost didn't hear it, so I kissed lower, tracing the vee of his pelvic muscles with my tongue and then swirling it around the tip of his cock, gently as I could.

Dante groaned, his hips bucking up, trying to push inside my mouth.

"Now, now," I said. "If you were going to be impatient you shouldn't have given me control."

Ironic. If I was in his position I'd be whining and begging with no dignity at all. But because I'm in control, I can wait as long as I need to...

I pressed his hip down with my palm and pinned it to the bed, slowly licking up and down his shaft.

"Ohhh, Cedric, fuck..."

"And you really shouldn't have let me tie you down if you don't like to be teased."

I slipped my hand down to play with his balls, gently rolling them in my fingers as I took him into my mouth again, savouring the taste of his dripping need.

"You are a demon without remorse," Dante said, his voice cracking. "We should call *you* Lucifer."

I chuckled around him and started to bob my head, sliding my lips up and down the silky length of him.

I dragged this out for a while longer, enjoying each shudder that passed through him, the way he'd gently press his hips against my palm and then subside at the slightest pressure from me.

Finally, I couldn't ignore the throbbing in my own cock any longer. I slicked up my fingers and started to stretch him open. "You've done very well, and I'm going to fuck you now."

Dante's mouth was open, and he was breathing heavily, his eyes half closed as he watched me working him. "Yes, please."

I grinned and lined my cock up against him, pressing slowly inside him. I leaned down on my hands, giving him another kiss as I slowly buried myself inside him. There was a slight quiver from the arm that had been injured but I ignored it, focusing on the more pleasant sensations.

A little high on the power, and the way he was squeezing me, I pulled back to watch his face, marvelling at the expression of pure delight. I was giving him that. His arms were pale, pulled up taut over his head, but he looked utterly relaxed.

I pressed deep inside and moaned. I decided I was done prolonging the foreplay, I wanted to get it all happening. I moved my knees up a little so I could start to thrust and properly fuck into him.

"Mmm, sunshine, yes," Dante opened his eyes and watched me as I moved, one of my hands braced on the bed beside his shoulder, the other stroking down his body to stroke his cock.

I liked that nickname too much to try and insist he call me sir or anything. Sunshine would work just fine for the two of us.

"Tell me Dante, are you hungry?" I asked, licking my lips with anticipation of the feeling of his fangs. I wanted it as much as he did.

I saw his Adam's apple bob and he nodded. "Please, yes, sunshine, please."

"Ask nicely," I said, grinning. I let go of his cock and lifted my arm in front of his mouth. "I'll only let you have it if you ask politely."

Dante breathed out, and I wondered if I'd finally pushed him to be annoyed with me, but he swallowed.

"Please, Sunshine, please may I feed from you?" His voice was liquid chocolate, warm, delicious and utterly irresistible.

I pressed the inside of my wrist to his mouth. "Go ahead, sweetheart."

His sharp teeth sank in and I gasped with the heat of it. My hips bucked and I thrust deep inside and orgasmed as I felt the tug and pull of Dante drinking from me. He was filled with me in two ways, and I felt like in that moment I was his whole world.

I loved that feeling.

He bucked under me and orgasmed, his voice muffled in my arm. The way his body rippled and clenched on me, I could almost come again, I thought. Almost.

I thrust a couple more times and then eased out of him as he opened his mouth and licked at the wound he'd made. I took a moment to watch his face, enjoying the sharp angle of his cheekbones, the blade of his jawbone.

"You're so incredibly handsome," I murmured.

"Thank you," he said, softly. "You're incandescent."

I reached up to tug the knots of the ropes undone. "That's a beautiful thing to say." I kissed him, tasting a slight iron tang of my own blood on his tongue.

Once he was freed, he wrapped his arms around me and pulled me close against his chest.

"I love you," Dante said, soft, his voice gravelly.

I swallowed, because I didn't know what I was feeling for him if it wasn't love, but to say it to him felt so raw. Frightening.

I was all right telling Oliver that, well, way back in London. I guess I hadn't said it a lot to him since... But he knew. How I felt for Dante wasn't quite the same as how I felt for Oliver, but... perhaps it wasn't so different either. And then there was how I felt for Gabriel... which.

"You don't have to say it back," Dante said. His hand stroked softly down my back and I realised I'd tensed against him.

Silly really. Why should I be afraid of three small words when I might be killed by a cult?

And I am obsessed with Dante, and his fangs and his cheekbones.

"I guess, I don't know a whole lot about what love is," I said, slowly. "I generally just get really focused on people and want them... but I want you a lot, and I don't want to be without you." Dante's hand slowed on my back.

"You don't?"

"I don't. I like the way you look after me, and you know when the magic is around, and... you're just so gorgeous. I... So, yes, I don't know what it means for the future, but I love you too."

Having said it I felt as if the ship might suddenly sink into the ocean and for a few seconds my pulse roared in my ears, but then the feeling cleared, and the ship rocked a little but didn't sink and I was still there in Dante's arms, and he loved me, and I loved him.

He squeezed me close and kissed me like he'd never let me go.

My heart felt like it would swell out of my chest.

CHAPTER 27

IN WHICH SOME THINGS CHANGE

*T*hat evening, I had sort of intended to do another painting, but it didn't seem like the best idea, given the events of the last few days.

I went to sit on the bed in the privacy of Gabriel's cabin and I took out the witches' jar. It was sealed, and I had no interest in trying to break that seal, but I wanted to look at the little wooden figure inside.

I held the jar up to the light, peering through the herbs and ash to see the figurine. Only it didn't look exactly how I remembered it. In fact, it seemed to have changed shape slightly. The head wasn't as round or as ... human shaped. It sort of looked like it had elongated.

I felt cold sweat bead on my forehead and my fingers shook slightly. I set the jar down on the bed and took a deep, steadying breath. Probably it was just a trick of the light, right?

It was made of wood, it couldn't just mutate.

But it was wood that... came to me in a dream and then I had it in real life somehow. The thing was magic so as far as I knew there were no rules about what it could and couldn't do.

I sighed and picked up the jar again, turned it this way and that, but yes. It had changed. The shape of the head was more oval, stretching up.

What should I do? I should tell the others, of course.

But we've only just arrived in this place ready to rest and hide for a while. It would be a pity to upset them...

And it's not like we can just leave and find a witch, we are hiding to stop being seen.

But it would be irresponsible to hide if the curse is somehow getting worse. I can't keep this to myself.

Sighing, I pocketed the jar and went out onto the deck. Gabriel had his spyglass in hand and was looking towards the West. I could see from the tension in his shoulders that he wasn't looking about for fun.

"Aye, I see it," he called. There was a response from Bilal who was up the mast, on watch.

"They've not seen us," they called back. "But I'd wager my left arm they're looking for us."

Gabriel sighed mightily and lowered the glass. "Well, the idea was to not be seen."

Bilal was down the rigging and beside him in flash, I approached too but felt uneasy about bringing up my problem when there was possibly another bounty hunter attack imminent.

"They don't appear willing to enter the channel, as you suspected," Bilal said. "Although they may chance it if they see us."

At least we're well enough hidden, I suppose." Gabriel turned to me. "Yes, Cedric?"

"Oh uh, I just have something to uh, show you, but it can wait."

Gabriel raised an eyebrow and then nodded. "Fine. I need to decide on our next course of action, we can't sit here forever."

Dante ambled up to our small group with a map in his hand. "I've been thinking of those things we heard in Tortuga about St

Vincent," he said. "The bounties were raised shortly after the evidence of large magic was seen there. It could be related."

Gabriel cocked his head to the side. "It could be, or it could be nothing to do with it. It seems like an arbitrary cause and effect you've put together there."

"Perhaps," Dante said. "But we know Natalia Harrow survived, she escaped us in Casablanca and I do not believe she'd have paused in her pursuit of Cedric. She needs him, his tattoo, for their dread rituals. We also know she can use magic, or she knows how to find people who can. We've heard of a large and highly unusual display of magic. I think it bears investigating."

"I'll think about it," Gabriel said. "For now, let's tell the crew to keep it down until that ship has gone. Bilal, get back up there and keep an eye out, will you?"

"Aye, Cap'n." I watched Bilal scale the mast and climb to a high yardarm with some amount of awe. I'd never so much as tried to climb a rigging in my life, and I wasn't about to start now. But I could still appreciate the skill on display.

In a couple of hours the ship was gone, and that night Gabriel sent Marco out to do some reconnaissance in otter form. To scout if there were other ships nearby, see if he could overhear anything.

Dinner was subdued that night and Dante slept in his own cabin. I slept beside Gabriel but we didn't do much more than cuddle. I was mostly asleep and he was snoring when I realised I'd forgotten about the figure in the jar. It seemed unfair to wake him up, so I resolved to tell him in the morning.

In the morning Marco returned to the ship and reported to Gabriel as we were eating breakfast together.

"No ships close enough to find us. The merfolk are avoiding us though, and when I found one who was willing to talk they said it was because of the wicked curse we were carrying aboard," Marco said. He had the decency to look sheepish as he related this news.

I flushed. "I don't suppose they meant the merfolk in the brig, did they?"

Marco frowned sympathetically and I dropped my eyes to the eggs on my plate. I didn't feel like finishing them.

The jar!

"Uh, speaking of curses," I mumbled, looking up and around for Dante. "I have some unsettling news."

Dante caught my eye from where he'd been listening to our conversation with Bilal, and it gave me a little courage to continue to speak.

"Unsettling?" Gabriel asked. He looked at me in a less sympathetic manner to Dante, but I had started this now and I was going to finish it.

"Right yes, the witches' jar."

"You didn't break it did you?" Gabriel interjected.

"No, please give me a little credit. It's still sealed and everything. It's just I was looking in it, and the wooden figure appears... changed."

There was silence over the group and in fact, over the whole ship. I could hear with clarity the lapping of gentle waves on the side of the ship.

"Changed." Gabriel repeated.

"Might I see it?" Dante was by my side, his expression warm, but concerned.

My mouth had gone quite dry, as if admitting that there was a problem out loud had instantly made the problem a lot worse. Perhaps it had, because now I had to deal with it.

I pulled out the jar and showed it to Dante. He turned it this way and that in his hand, peering in. Oliver looked over his shoulder and even Bilal leaned in.

My shoulders twitched and I shifted my weight, feeling vastly uncomfortable as they examined the jar with such intensity.

Part of me was relieved that they could see something worthy of examination, it meant I hadn't just imagined it. However, if I had imagined it, perhaps it would have been more of a relief.

Dante finally handed it back to me. He looked at me briefly and then fixed his eyes on the captain. "This is not good news."

Gabriel rubbed the bridge of his nose. "I hardly thought it would be good news, Dante."

"We need to get to the source of this curse and cut it off," he said. "St Vincent is our only lead, Captain, please."

My heart sped up and I looked to Gabriel who sighed again and then nodded. "Fine, we sail for St Vincent, but we have to assume as soon as our ship is sighted, if Harrow is there, she will send whoever she has to attack us."

"Indeed," Dante said. He rested a hand on my knee and looked at me as if I had just received some kind of fatal diagnosis. Perhaps I had, in a way.

"Fine, we sail. We make preparations and we assume this is some kind of trap," Gabriel said. "Bilal, please go up the mast again and check the way is clear. Dante... what do you suggest we do with our prisoner?"

Oliver cleared his throat. "Uh, with all due respect, Captain. Perhaps Scratch could help us. They were hunting us after all, perhaps that would be a safe way into port without being fired on, assuming Harrow is, as you say, there."

Gabriel gazed at Oliver for a moment and then nodded slowly. "Would they agree to that, do you think?"

Oliver nodded. "Oh yes, captain, they've been quite affable

these last few days. They say that things under the sea are so horrid they don't really mind the idea of joining a pirate ship."

"Huh," I said, without really meaning to. I knew Oliver had spent a good deal of time studying the merfolk but I had imagined his line of questioning to be a lot more scientific. It sounded like he'd made friends with the mer.

"It's possible they're lulling you into trusting them for some other reason," Gabriel said. "But it could be worth a try anyway. They know that a bite from Dante will subdue them after all, we have that weapon up our sleeve."

"Could be," Oliver said, genially. "I'll speak to them about it anyway, if you like."

Gabriel nodded and sighed and looked at me again. "And what will we do with you?"

I spread my hands in what I hoped was a winning way and shrugged.

CHAPTER 28

IN WHICH THE CREW MAKES A PLAN

The voyage to St Vincent constituted a week or so sailing South, closer and closer to the equator. In that time Gabriel formulated a plan with the help of the rest of us.

We would approach the island of St Vincent, pretend that Scratch had caught the ship, in particular the Captain and Quartermaster, and gain access to whoever had set the bounty. If it was Natalia Harrow then we could hopefully do something to break the curse. If it wasn't her, well, the source of the high bounties would be removed.

It was a picturesque voyage, and I had two nights in Oliver's bed, which set me in a better mood. The voyage was also curiously free of attacks from bounty hunters.

"Could be that they know we're coming towards them," Gabriel said.

"If they're tracking the ship then yes, they will know that," Dante said. "I don't think anyone on the ship is informing them of the goings on, or anything like that."

Both of them looked at me uneasily, and I shrugged. "Just uh, I'm just doing the best I can with the jar and the tattoo and everything. I haven't dreamed anything about telling anyone if that's a comfort?"

"We're not blaming you," Gabriel said. "They've been pursuing the ship, not you, since we got the jar."

Either way, the voyage was easy compared to how things had been. We even took a day to hide some treasure and other valuables on a deserted island, so that if the cult did overrun the ship as part of our plan, they wouldn't bankrupt us.

I got to make a proper pirate treasure map to record the exact location of the booty, which all felt very swashbuckling and buccaneer-ish.

Scratch the merfolk had agreed to assist in this ruse and had even been allowed up on deck in a probationary way, shackled, to ensure that they wouldn't sing or start killing at the first opportunity. But indeed, they seemed to be rather friendly now, as Oliver had said.

"Regular food sure helps," they said, when Marco commented on their friendliness.

"It really does," Marco agreed.

Gabriel insisted they stay in the brig at night, but soon Scratch was a regular fixture on the deck, unshackled, and learning the ways of the ship. I spent a good two hours one afternoon watching them learn knots from Dante. Scratch's muscles were thick and their arms were as wide as my thighs. It was very stirring indeed.

Gabriel had made it clear they were on a sort of trial run, and had them paired with Dante for a lot of the day, but to me it genuinely seemed that Scratch was willing to change and be included.

I wondered if they'd also be willing to experiment with fucking me, but decided to wait until this whole thing in St Vincent was done before I suggested it.

We sailed into the port at Kingstown, St Vincent. The island itself was a lot bigger and more mountainous than many I'd seen in the Caribbean. It appeared to be mostly jungle with a couple of towns on the outskirts. Stunningly beautiful and verdant greens that sang out to be painted, but now wasn't the time.

A small boat seemed to follow us into the mooring, which felt rather ominous, but perhaps was to be expected. If the cult had overrun this little port, then we could assume that everyone was an enemy after all.

Someone on the docks helped to tie up the ship, and Gabriel gave us all a nod before gesturing for Scratch to go first and then stepping lightly down the gangplank.

Dante and I followed close behind. We'd barely stepped off the marina when a man in an impressive looking hat and a coat with shiny buttons on it appeared in our path. There were five men with him, in coats with less buttons than the main one had.

The man in the hat cleared his throat and intoned loudly.

"Captain Lucifer, you are under arrest," he said. "By order of the governor of Saint Vincent you are to be brought in immediately."

"Scuse me," Scratch said. "But I captured these pirates, and I've brought them here for my bounty. You can't just arrest them."

"Hm," the man eyed Scratch and shifted his weight from one foot to the other.

"Yes, fine, all right," Gabriel said. He nodded a little at the man, who seemed surprised that he hadn't put up a fight.

The man gestured to his posse and they moved forward, brandishing swords that weren't as fancy or shiny as the ones Gabriel used. "You'll need to be surrendering any weapons, then. You too, Mister Gregoros."

"It's Grigorios," Dante said, dryly. "Obviously we are not armed, since this bounty hunter has brought us in."

The men eyed me next and one of them nudged the other and they both approached. "Are you armed?"

Although this was all part of the plan, and I had got off the ship in order to be part of this group that was taken in, a part of me wanted nothing more than to bolt and save myself.

I glanced over my shoulder at the safety of the Devil's Whore, and saw that it was being cast off. On the deck, Oliver watched with a stony expression, while Marco and the others worked to get the sails unfurled.

I swallowed, looked back at the men arresting us and shook my head. "No, I'm not."

All the same the man frisked me, his hands moving quickly to pat me down, and of course, inevitably, he found the witch's jar.

"I'll be taking this." I made as if to take it back, my heart starting to race with a more real fear that my protection would be removed.

"Please, it's-"

"Stay quiet, Cedric," Dante said, sharply and I bit my tongue.

Yes, of course, best not to give them more information than they already had.

There was a clanking of chains and I saw the men were shackling Gabriel and Dante but for me they produced a large iron ring. It hinged open and as they brought it towards me I realised it was a collar. Like you'd use for a slave, or someone condemned to die.

"Miss Harrow said you were a slippery one, Mister Hale-Harrington," one of the men said, as they settled the heavy thing around my neck and padlocked it shut. It sat loose, not cutting into my throat, but it had a chain attached to it like a leash and I had no doubt they'd yank on it if I didn't follow behind. It was a substantial weight on my shoulders.

In another circumstance, I might have been sort of fascinated with it, but it wasn't the time or place for thoughts of what Gabriel would do to me if he had me in this thing.

I had to try and keep my wits about me.

They led us to a waiting carriage and bundled us inside. I was careful to watch the feet of the man at the other end of my chain so I didn't lag at all.

The carriage took us up to a house on the hill. It rather reminded me of the kind of English villa the governor of Jamaica kept. Impressive, nice views.

Of course, we didn't get a long time to admire the place as Natalia Harrow waited within.

CHAPTER 29

IN WHICH A POWERFUL NAME IS LEARNED,
AND A RITUAL COMMENCED

*D*ante and Gabriel were taken one way and I was led another, Scratch came with us although the men hadn't said anything to them.

Up a grand staircase they led me and to a large room which looked out over the city. There was almost no furniture in the room, although the chandelier was rather pretty. There was a low chaise in one corner, but otherwise it appeared to be empty.

Natalia Harrow stood silhouetted against the large window, apparently waiting for me.

The man leading me cleared his throat. "Mistress Harrow, we've brought you the boy."

"Actually, I brought you two pirates and I'd like the reward, thanks," Scratch said, their voice ringing and clear in the room, bouncing off the marble flagstones.

Natalia turned then, and eyed Scratch with a false smile. "I don't know what you're referring to," she said.

Scratch closed the distance between them with a few short strides, growling. "Don't mess with me, lady. You're the one who's been hiring bounty hunters and I'm the one who came through. I want my reward, and if you don't give it to me, I'll start singing."

It was a very convincing performance. Perhaps Scratch had planned this all along and they'd simply take the reward and go? Leave us to whatever mercy Harrow had and make their own way in the world again with the substantial money?

I could hardly blame them if they did.

"And apparently this boy is worth something to you as well, so you can compensate me for him as well."

Scratch had a good foot on Natalia, and although I could see her nostrils flare, she kept her composure incredibly well with the buff merfolk looming over her. Perhaps she had seen more frightening things in her time.

"Right, yes, of course. Follow me to the office and I'll compensate you."

She started to walk towards the door and caught my eye as two more people entered the room. Her face split into a smug smile. "Cedric, dear, go with Miss Tilighast and Mr Muncheim here and we'll get you into something more fitting for the ritual tonight."

I last saw Scratch following Natalia into a room with a large desk in it. My new captors took me in another direction, to a guest room. They were rather more well dressed and refined looking than the men who had met us at the docks. Miss Tilighast had a fine gown of deepest blue on, and Mr Muncheim wore something very like the latest fashion I'd seen in the window of the best suitmakers in London.

"What happened to the governor?" I asked Miss Tilighast. "Surely Natalia isn't the governor."

"No, lad, the governor is downstairs. Well, in the ground downstairs. You don't need to worry. Now, come along, we must commence preparing for the ritual." She gave me a smile that stretched her pretty lips wide and displayed what felt like too many teeth. I felt a familiar flutter of revulsion as I remembered the last ritual I'd been involved in, which was exacerbated by the toothiness of the smile.

"Of course, the uh, yes, the ritual," I said.

Miss Tilighast pointed at a robe laid out on the bed and nodded encouragingly. Muncheim stood nearby with the end of the chain held loosely in his hand, as if I were a misbehaving dog and he was waiting to see what I'd do, ready with the choke chain.

"Go on, get changed, darling boy."

"I thought there was a ceremonial bathing," I said, stalling for time. "Are you sure you want me in that thing, or in the ritual with all my sea salt and grime still attached? Won't that, you know, ruin the look of the thing? I'm pretty sure there's a ceremonial bath."

The two of them looked at each other with a fair amount of uncertainty. "Uh, well," Muncheim said, and I thought he was coming around to my way of thinking but Miss Tilighast shook her head.

"No Andal, Elder Harrow didn't say anything about bathing him, and her orders are to be followed, not improvised with."

"Right." Andal Muncheim nodded once, sharply, and pointed at me. "Get changed then, will you? I don't mind helping if needed but you might as well do it yourself."

"So, this ritual," I said, starting to undo my shirt but not exactly being speedy about it. "It's to summon the big thing, right?"

"Big... thing?" Muncheim repeated.

"Yeah, you know," I said. I thought back reluctantly to the images from my dreams. "The uh, gentleman who resides behind the stars? I can't recall his name just now, but I'm sure the two of you know it, fine upstanding folks like yourselves."

"Of course I know," Muncheim said. "It's whatshisname. Father of our friend. It's hard to pronounce their names, though."

"And sort of bad luck, as I understand it" Miss Tilighast added. "Like seeing the bride right before the wedding ceremony or something like that."

"I mean," I said, forcing an idle laugh that masked a healthy amount of nervousness. Or at least, I hoped it masked it. "No one's getting married to this... thing, right?"

"No, of course not, darling," Miss Tilighast laughed with me, her laugh was charmingly musical, like a peal of small bells. "Azathoth isn't coming to our world to take a bride, what a notion! No, it will bring with it a reckoning."

My mouth went bone dry at the sound of that word.

The name echoed in my ears and shuddered through my bones.

Azathoth... Azathoth... Azathoth...

I'd never heard a word like it. But some part of me, perhaps the cursed part, recognised it. I saw, before my eyes as if I were dreaming again, the stars parting and something moving closer. The thump of tentacles behind me.

I felt cold, and I could smell a sort of ozone scent, the ocean and lightning both.

I dropped my shirt from trembling hands, unable to speak or think aside from the thought of that thing. That Azathoth, coming closer to me from beyond the firmament.

Appearing in my painting... calling to me through dreams, through whatever means it could...

Surprisingly gentle hands helped me into the ceremonial robe and I didn't realise it was happening until I came back to myself. It was as if I'd been in a trance.

"That's it, now step out of your trousers, dearest," Miss Tilighast said. "Then we'll get the oil on you."

That snapped me out of the reverie I'd been in since hearing that name.

My body reacted violently before I could form a coherent thought. I shoved against the two of them and backed away, quickly finding the reach of the chain and not caring at all at the way it pressed against the bones in the back of my neck.

"No! No oil, not that. Keep that away from me!"

They both looked at me in surprise. I glanced down and saw that I was quite naked although I couldn't remember getting that way.

I guessed I'd been rather docile, moving without thinking for a good few minutes, and this reaction had startled them.

"Well, perhaps it's best if we leave it for Natalia, after all." Muncheim said.

"Just stay calm, now, Chosen One," Miss Tilighast said.

They hadn't been calling me that before, had they? No, I think that was new since they'd... said the name. I felt my mind recoiling from the knowledge of it, shying back from even speaking it inside my head as if it were dangerous, poison. And perhaps it was.

"Just Cedric is fine," I muttered. I brought a hand up to the chain where it attached to the iron collar, as if I thought I could loosen it or something foolish like that. Perhaps I just wanted to make believe I had some sort of control over the situation.

"Here, slip this on," Muncheim brought a ceremonial robe towards me, and I found I did want to cover myself. I let him help me into it.

"Darling boy, Cedric, you've done so well," Miss Tilighast said. "Now that you're dressed, we ought to go downstairs. Everyone will be waiting for you."

It wasn't like I had any kind of choice. Muncheim and Tilighast ushered me down the stairs and into a side chamber holding fast to the chain which was locked around my neck. Inside were a small bevy of hooded figures, a wooden X shape standing upright in the centre of the floor, and Natalia Harrow, a robe pulled over her shoulders, and her hood pushed down to reveal an impressive black dress of shiny brocade, embroidered here and there with little silver stars.

My stomach turned over unpleasantly.

Stars... oh stars, I really hope our plan works and she doesn't gut me.

"Natalia," I said, lifting my chin up and grinning like I owned the place, even though I was being led in on a chain like a dog. "How lovely to see you again."

"Lovely indeed," Natalia said. She nodded towards the wooden cross. It was supported on a heavy wooden base with struts and everything. I imagined it could hold rather a lot of weight.

"Shouldn't there be some kind of protective circle?" I asked. "Or are you lot all perfectly happy to be eaten first?"

"Leave the magic to the experts."

"Remind me, won't you, Miss Harrow, what exactly it is we're doing here tonight?" I said. I dug my heels in a little so Miss Tilighast would stop trying to haul me in the direction of the cross. "You see, the thing is, that I'm often invited to these little soirées, but I'm rather kept in the dark as to their purpose, if you get my meaning."

"Oh, Chosen One," Natalia moved closer to me, raised a hand and gently caressed my cheek. I tried not to flinch away but there was a slight movement, I couldn't prevent. I saw her eyes narrow and she slapped my cheek. Not hard enough to snap my head to the side, but enough to sting. "You don't *need* to know our purpose here, you just need to be present, and bleed the right blood."

"The right blood?" I swallowed, my heart thumping so loud and so quickly all of a sudden that it was thrumming in my ears. "What's my blood got to do with it?"

"You didn't think we'd have put this darling on just anyone, do you?" Her fingers trailed down my shoulder and over my shoulder blade, in a hideous parody of intimacy. I couldn't help myself, I shuddered as her fingers touched the tattoo. She must have noticed this, but she didn't react. She held out her hand, and Muncheim placed the jar of oil into it.

"So, what's your quarrel with me?" I asked. I made to step towards Miss Tilighast, but she moved in and clamped her free hand around my arm, holding me in place.

"Not with you, darling one," Tilighast said.

"Your line," Natalia Harrow said. She moved, slithered, almost, to the side. There was a pause as she poured the oil out into her hand and began to gently slather it over the expanse of my back. I could feel the tattoo start to awaken, and my mind tried to avoid knowing that.

"What about my line?"

"Talkative sort, isn't' he?" A man pushed his hood back from his face, and moved closer, peering into my eyes. He didn't have the air of deference to Natalia Harrow that the others displayed, and he was uncommonly tall. Far taller and thinner than Gabriel was... His arms seemed far too long as he reached out towards me, cupping my chin in his hands. I shook my head, dislodging his grip but only for a moment.

He had sandy, almost red hair, cropped short, bright pale sky blue eyes and a smile that seemed to stretch over half his face. I felt myself wanting to smile back at him.

"Perhaps we should gag him," Natalia said. "But I was looking forward to hearing his screams. He has such a fine voice when he gets going."

"Oh will you *shut up*?" Marco said, pushing his hood down and moving forward, sword raised.

CHAPTER 30

IN WHICH THE RITUAL IS SOMEWHAT DISRUPTED

I was peering into the face of the tall man when this happened, so I got to enjoy the look of abject confusion on his face. He straightened to his full height, which must have been close to seven feet, his face a picture of consternation as he stalked with long strides towards Marco.

Natalia Harrow shoved me forwards, pressing me bodily against the wooden cross and grazing the exposed skin. I was distracted from that pain by the twisting sensation on my back.

Natalia was doing something with the chain and the cross, and then I saw the flash of a knife in her hand, felt white hot pain as she sliced my arm, before she was pulled off me.

I twisted, catching myself. Natalia had secured the chain to the cross, leaving me a scant foot of wiggle room. But this was enough to face out, and see that the crew of the Devil's Whore had pulled off the plan admirably. Marco had his sword to Natalia's throat, Oliver had a sword aimed at the tall man, his robe pushed back to reveal charmingly dishevelled hair and a triumphant grin, and Bilal had dispatched two more cultists in the corner.

I looked down at my arm to see a shallow cut across the forearm. My blood dripped onto the ground.

Dante and Gabriel walked in, unfettered, with Scratch by their sides, all three of them armed again.

"You didn't wait for us?" Dante asked, his tone sardonic. He caught Natalia Harrow's eye and she hissed at him.

"She was going to do something with that knife," Marco said. "Thought it best not to wait around."

"Indeed." Gabriel stalked forward and picked up the knife that Natalia Harrow had dropped. He looked at me. His eyes possibly lingered for a second on the collar, chain and cross situation, but to his credit he didn't appear distracted. "Did they hurt you?"

I shook my head. "A cut here but it's already stopped bleeding and, Captain, they just... did the oil thing again. My back, the tattoo..." and I didn't say any more because the tattoo twisted itself and I felt the awful searing pain I had hoped never to feel again.

"Now, let's not be hasty," the tall man said, moving a little closer to me, although Oliver made a warning noise and brought his sword closer to the man's throat, he halted, but didn't seem too concerned at all. "We've started something here, after all. The Chosen One's blood has been spilt."

"You've started something that will not be completed," Gabriel said. "How do we remove the tattoo?" He looked between Natalia and the tall man, his expression fierce. "Tell me, or I slit your throat."

"You can't remove it," Natalia said, her voice delighted. "It's magically applied, and it's there for one purpose, to open a way for the Unknowable One."

"For Azathoth," the tall man said. His eyes lit with an unearthly light and I cringed back against the cross. He pinched the flat of Oliver's blade between his thumb and forefinger and plucked it from his hand, which shouldn't have been possible, since Oliver was strong and had a firm grip. I couldn't make sense of it.

Further, the word Azathoth was echoing in my head again. My eyesight swam as if I had been plunged underwater and the figures in the room blurred.

I blinked frantically, even brought my hand up to my eyes to wipe at them, but when I opened my eyes again the room had darkened, and I could see the stars.

"That can't be," I muttered to myself. "I'm inside, there are no stars here."

"Cedric? Can you hear me?" Oliver's voice was beside me, close. I fancied I could feel his warm, steady hand on my arm. I blinked again and the room became clearer. The ceiling, the people. The tall man, stalking his way towards Gabriel, who raised his sword defensively.

Natalia Harrow squirmed in Marco's grasp and produced something, held it aloft and smashed it onto the ground. It shattered, glass. I shook my head and peered, trying to understand, although my heart was racing and I thought I knew... my glass jar. The witch's protection. It was destroyed.

"Cedric, listen to me, you have to focus," Oliver said. There was a jangling sound, he was trying to free me perhaps?

I closed my eyes to blink and found it hard to reopen them.

I felt a cool wind on my cheek. The smell of rotten seaweed and wood left in the ocean to disintegrate.

I opened my eyes to find myself on the deck of a ship. There was no chain on me, and above my head the stars were dancing.

Oliver's voice was gone, there was no one there. I was alone with the stars, and the magic, and whatever it was that lived behind the stars.

Azathoth.

I thought the word, or perhaps I spoke it out loud, because it seemed to echo back at me, from the ocean waves, from the stars, from the boards beneath my feet. An echo which was also a vibration.

The stars began to part and I saw something strange behind

them. Lit with the silver starlight, it appeared to have large tentacles, but it wasn't shaped like an octopus. It was far too large and strange to fully comprehend.

Azathoth.

It was coming.

CHAPTER 31

IN WHICH CEDRIC BATTLES ALONE

*L*ooking back over the times I've got into fisticuffs, I had to reflect that I've never been what one might call a fighter.

I mean, I'd gotten into my fair share of bar brawls and so on, but that was while bolstered with alcohol and hardly included any kind of skill.

The pirates kept me out of the fights on the ship, and although it was frustrating, it was probably fair enough. The fact was that I knew which end of the sword to hold, but the fencing lessons I'd had to take at school had more or less vanished from my memory as soon as the class was passed.

So, here I found myself alone and with no way to fight whatever was coming for me. Whatever Azathoth was. God? Demon? Something entirely else?

Was this even real? I asked myself. A second ago I'd felt Oliver's hand on me. I'd seen Gabriel.

It felt real. I could feel the wooden boards beneath my feet, they felt real enough.

Unlike in the dreams, I found I could look around, I wasn't stuck staring at the stars. I turned in place, seeing the railings of a ship, the ocean beyond it. There wasn't a lot of detail, there were no sails on the mast, no ropes lying about or barrels on the deck. The ocean stretched into the horizon on every side, dark and choppy.

I remembered the strange noises of something approaching me from behind in the dreams, but there was nothing that appeared to have gained access to the deck.

... yet.

Instead there was me, and the dread presence overhead.

My protection was gone. Whatever spell the witches had cast around me and my little wooden effigy was destroyed, and there was oil on my back, and my tattoo... it was moving.

It occurred to me that it wasn't hurting me the way it normally did, that was something good.

I'm here in a dream space, which may or may not be real, my protection is gone, and I have no one to help me.

I wonder if I can handle this alone?

I hope back in the real world Gabriel has stabbed Natalia Harrow. And that weird tall man. His eyes were magical, I think.

Azathoth was above, and drawing nearer.

There's nothing I can do, I realised. My eyes slid up and I tried to make sense of the horror I saw there. The form Azathoth took seemed to shift and blur, not allowing my mind to settle on a definitive answer for what it was.

Dread flooded my body like ice water. My teeth began to rattle against each other, and my mind spun with the hopelessness of it all.

What could someone like me do against... that?

Our plan had been to stop the cultists before it got too far. We were going to get some information, Gabriel would stab some people, Dante would feed, and we'd get out of there without anything like this happening.

But it had happened.

And now I was here, all alone. I felt my knees buckle,

threatening to give out. What would happen if I did? If I just... let it all overwhelm me and collapse?

I eyed the deck. I could. I could just give up. I didn't have the first idea of how to fight back or cope with any of this.

It was too much for me. I was just... me. I was just the rich, spoiled son of a politician and I had no idea what to do.

If I did give up, what would happen?

The thing would use my back... it would use the tattoo and come through into our world, the real world.

And then what would it do? I couldn't imagine that it would sit down to tea and biscuits. No, what had Miss Tilighast said?

'It will bring about a reckoning.'

It would eat things, probably, destroy. Possibly tear apart everything I knew and loved about the world. I thought of the horror I'd felt when it had appeared in my painting. The gut wrenching fear.

Azathoth would bring that fear, that horror, to all who saw it. And it hardly seemed like the Cult of the Unknowable way wanted to contain it, they seemed joyful, didn't they? They wanted it to come through and do... whatever it would do.

I tried to think back to what the first Harrow had said to me, but my head ached with a sudden, sharp pain. I glanced up to see a tentacle wrap around a star, the monstrous thing, the beast, pulling itself closer.

This fussing and wondering isn't helping anything, Cedric, I said to myself as sternly as I could. I imagined it was Gabriel saying it to me, or Oliver, perhaps. *Get your act together and do something.*

"Right, yes, all right," I said, out loud. "I will do something." It felt good to say it out loud. My back itched but I ignored it.

I had to do something. What was it Natalia had said? That I could open the way for it? Or that my tattoo could. Well, my tattoo was part of me, wasn't it?

I tried to summon up some courage, or at the very least, an

idea of what to do. If I had any kind of magical power, it would have been useful just then.

You just have yourself, and that's all.

No magic.

No sword. Although, what did I think I'd do with a sword? Wave it at the sky until the eldritch beast got close enough? There was no way that could work.

I looked back up at Azathoth and shouted as loud as I could. "Fuck off! Just bugger off, will you? We don't want you around here!"

Its large, central eye swivelled around and then fixed itself on me. For a moment I was frozen in place.

All right, yelling directly at it doesn't seem to be the way forward. Think of something else, Cedric. Think!

After a moment I tore my eyes away from Azathoth's and cast around again. The deck was a lot more bare than the Devil's Whore, but it wasn't empty entirely. There was the railing...

I strode over to the railing of the ship. Without meaning to, I glanced into the ocean and saw it roiling with... things. More monsters, tentacles and strange people with large, protruding eyes and wide frog-like mouths. There were so many, countless numbers of them and I felt myself beginning to freeze up again.

"No, no, I'm doing something," I said, through gritted teeth. I seized the railing with both hands and started to rotate it, trying to unscrew it or something similar. It rolled in my fingers but didn't seem to be coming loose at all. "Come on, you stupid thing, come on. I'm going to tear this whole place apart, and see what happens then."

It came off in my hands, and I threw it into the ocean.

I went to the next bit of railing and yanked it loose, it came apart like cardboard or hard bread, chunks falling apart in my hands. For a few frenzied minutes I tore and spat, pulling the ship apart with an ease that shouldn't have been possible.

My back was itching where the tattoo was, but it was

warming me as well. It was almost as if the tattoo was urging me on.

Perhaps it was.

If it was urging me on, did that mean I was on the right track? Or was I doing as Azathoth wanted and speeding up the proceedings?

Well, I didn't have any better plan. I bent and hauled the boards of the deck up, tossing them behind me in my frenzy to destroy it all.

Finally I took a rest, my heart was thumping but less with fear and more from exhilaration. I glanced up to see Azathoth had stalled, it hadn't moved closer.

"Don't like that?" I yelled, feeling almost light-headed now. High on the success, or maybe the destruction. "Yeah, well, fuck you! I'm going to tear this whole thing apart and then what will happen?"

I gestured at the thing in the stars, the middle finger so that it would know the extent of the contempt I felt for it. My back warmed, as if hot oil flowed through my veins from the heat on my back. I felt hot and silver light flooded me, something I had never felt before.

It felt incredible. Not just good, but powerful. As if the magic from the tattoo was now mine to control.

I took a deep breath and gestured again, this time pushing the flat of my palm towards the thing in the sky. "Fuck you!"

To my amazement, a bronze light, metallic and unnatural poured out of my hand. It arced up towards the stars, towards Azathoth, and I actually saw it flinch. It was the tiniest movement, but it filled me with incredible confidence.

The tattoo was part of me, I'd been trying to avoid that truth for weeks, since I first discovered it. I'd been trying to get rid of it, trying to do something to counteract it. But that was the wrong approach. Instead, I should have embraced it. How foolish I had been!

Now I welcomed it wholeheartedly, allowing the bronze light to fill me. I closed my eyes and laughed as I felt tingling from the tips of my fingers down to my toes.

When I opened my eyes again, the ship, which I had been tearing apart seemed a lot less real, far less solid. I thought I could probably slip back from this place, back to where the pirates were, and the cultists.

"Adieu, Azathoth you fucking hideous monster! You scurvy bilge rat!" I punctuated these insults with another blast of energy out of my hand and the world went dark.

CHAPTER 32

IN WHICH CEDRIC ENJOYS HIS NEW POWER

*J*opened my eyes and I was back in the ballroom with the others. Oliver's hand was on my shoulder, digging in his nails as if trying to rouse me.

I coughed once and looked up at Oliver who was peering at me with clear concern. I winked at him, a smile spreading over my face, because I could still feel the bronze coloured power inside me. My back was warm, pleasantly so, and I could feel the warmth in my limbs. My palms tingled with it.

"You're all right," Oliver said. He turned to call to Gabriel, who appeared to be about to run Natalia Harrow through. "Cedric woke up!"

I reached up and touched the collar, felt for the padlock and closed my fingers around it. I was testing to see if the power would in fact work in this place as well as in the dream realm or... wherever I had been.

I felt my fingers heat and the padlock metal cracked and snapped open. I eased the collar off my neck and left it hanging there.

"How did you..." Oliver breathed, his voice a little more frightened than impressed.

Gabriel had looked over at me, and in doing so his sword

tip had dipped towards the floor. Natalia broke free from Marco's grip on her arm and dashed towards me, shouting a word I didn't understand, but could feel the magic behind. A dagger, similar to the one she'd dropped earlier appeared in her hand. It was similar, but longer, and the blade curved back and forth in an insidious wave pattern. She raised it over her head.

"You will die!"

Oliver moved, as if to stand in front of me, but I pushed him aside, raised my palm and let the heat and the light flow through me. The bronze power arced out of my hand like an electrical surge, and struck her squarely in the chest. She tried to continue to run but the force from my blast struck her high, throwing her backwards so that she somersaulted in midair and landed heavily on the tiled floor.

Gabriel moved in to stab her prone form, but the tall man stopped him, clanging Oliver's sword against Gabriel's. They began to fight, parrying and thrusting over Natalia's prone body. She writhed a little, clearly in pain, and cursing me.

Behind them, the cultists seemed to take heart from the tall man's actions, and turned to fight the pirates, although they were outnumbered and definitely not as fierce.

I saw Miss Tilighast approaching Dante from behind and sent a blast of energy at her, knocking her off her feet.

Marco was attacking Muncheim with a series of swift chopping motions with his sword, and Muncheim was trying to defend himself with a dagger, and retreating towards the door.

I raised my hand to send a blast of power at the tall man, as he and Gabriel seemed quite evenly matched. I felt it build and flow down my arm just as the tall man glanced at me, shook his head and made a dismissive gesture with his free hand. This was all done at the same time he blocked a blow from Gabriel.

My power fizzled in my veins and my mouth went dry.

What on Earth was this man that he could do that to my power?

An incredibly powerful witch, perhaps. If that's what he was, why wasn't he running the cult instead of Natalia?

The tall man made a particularly vicious thrust with his sword, catching Gabriel on the sword arm so that he swore.

As Gabriel hesitated, shifting his sword into his other hand, the tall man bent, scooped up Natalia Harrow's wounded form and ran out of the room. His long legs ate up the distance to the door in just a few strides, even with Natalia over his shoulder. I tried to send a blast after the two of them but there was nothing.

Marco and Bilal followed after them, but I had a horrible feeling they wouldn't be able to catch the tall man.

Dante appeared beside me, wiping his mouth delicately on a handkerchief. "Cedric what did you do?"

"The tattoo," I said, a little breathless from the shock of having it and then the shock of losing it so quickly. "It's a part of me, I can use the magic within it."

"I'm not sure you should," Oliver said.

"It just saved me, using it," I said, a little affronted. "I saved us all."

"But the magic... If it comes from whatever it is they're trying to summon..." Oliver shook his head.

"All right, I think we're done here," Gabriel said. It looked as if all the cultists had been disposed of, save Miss Tilighast, and the two who had escaped. I went to her side and knelt down, she was awake, although stunned, and blinked at me slowly.

"Miss Tilighast. Hello. Who was the tall man? The one with the blue eyes who left with Harrow?"

A soft smile played over her lips and she reached a hand up to touch my cheek. I let her. "Why, he's the crawling chaos, the one who ushers in the true god."

I frowned. "I thought that was me, doesn't Aza..." now, back in the real world, I didn't feel confident saying the thing's name. "Doesn't the god come through me?"

She nodded, her fingers reaching back behind my ear and

pulling me down as if to kiss me, but instead she hissed in my ear. "You're the portal, the vessel, the thing we must use. But he is the high priest, the one who knows, the smiling man."

I pulled back, freeing myself of her grasp as she shuddered and then passed out. I wasn't entirely sure if she was dead or if I wanted her to be dead.

I stood up, shuddered bodily. I was reacting to her words, and my experience in the other realm. My back felt warm but not in the magical power sort of way, the rest of me was freezing. Gabriel had been watching and now he crossed to my side, slipping his arm around me.

"All right, Cedric?" I nodded weakly and he raised his voice, addressing the crew. "You all know what to do, take anything that might be worth something and let's head back to the ship."

Marco and Bilal came back empty handed.

"Did you kill Harrow?" Dante asked. They shook their heads.

"It was as if they vanished," Bilal said. "One moment I could see him carrying her and the next they were both gone."

The other pirates dispersed to search the villa, and even Oliver went off, too.

Gabriel took off his coat and slipped it over my shoulders, giving me a kiss on the forehead. "Are you all right?"

"I honestly don't know," I said.

CHAPTER 33

IN WHICH SOME THINGS ARE SETTLED AND SOME QUESTIONS ARE ASKED

The wooden figure found its way back into my pocket. It had three legs now, and there were strange protrusions from its head. I decided not to think too hard about that.

One thing I couldn't deny thinking about though was the tattoo. When we got back to the Devil's Whore, and I got myself out of the hideous robe and back into my clothes, which Dante had found and brought back for me, I noticed something on my shoulder. A black tentacle looking thing.

"Dante?" I called. He stepped into the cabin immediately, apparently he'd been waiting outside as if I needed privacy or something like that. I turned my back on him. "Dante has the tattoo got bigger? Because I rather suspect the tattoo has got bigger on account of I can see it on my shoulder and it used to be just on my back."

Dante put his hand on my waist, took his time formulating his response, which rather told me what the answer was.

"Yes," he said. "It's like it's stretched, the centre is larger, and the tentacles stretch further. Cedric, what happened back there?"

I turned and went to my toes, leaning up to plant a kiss on

his lips. "I'll get the others in, and I'll explain it to all of you. How about that?"

Dante nodded, kissed the top of my head and let go of me. "Perfect. I'm... honestly, I'm just so glad you're safe, sunshine. I thought they'd wait at least a few hours before they started any kind of ritual. It was as if they expected us, somehow."

That was another problem I'd have to ponder.

Out on the deck, the crew were sorting through the sacks of loot they'd liberated from the Governor's house. I eyed a side of roast beef with interest. Dinner was going to be especially good this evening...

Oliver was sitting to the side, flipping through the pages of a large leather bound book I didn't recognise.

"Oliver, would you come into the Captain's cabin? I want to explain what I saw," I said. He looked up and smiled uncertainly.

"Yes, all right. Uh, this book might help with the bits you don't understand," he said. He held up the cover and showed me the title. *The tenets of the Cult of the Unknowable Way.*

I went to find Gabriel next, which wasn't hard, as he was at the helm with Bilal. The ship was under sail and the island of St Vincent was already a small dot on the horizon.

He looked up as I approached, nodded to Bilal and came closer, meeting me halfway.

"Yes?"

"I thought we could all talk," I said. "About what happened to me."

He nodded and pressed his hand into the small of my back as I turned. Half comforting, half controlling. It was such an essentially Gabriel gesture I couldn't help but appreciate it.

Once all my lovers were assembled, Gabriel and Dante on the bed, side by side and looking a bit awkward about it, Oliver on the desk chair and me standing, facing them all, I began to speak.

"It wasn't like last time. Last time I felt like it was all happening just then, something in my back reaching for something... beyond. Today, I went back into the place I've had nightmares about..." and I detailed, as best I could, what I had seen. How I had yelled at Azathoth, although I shied away from saying the name out loud, and how I had realised I could use the magic in my back tattoo.

It was a part of me, and I had come to understand... a little bit of it at least. I told them everything, including the bit Oliver had witnessed, where I'd used my powers to destroy the lock. Of course they'd all seen me blast Natalia Harrow. But I told them what Miss Tilighast had said to me about the tall man. How she'd called him such a strange name.

Gabriel took a deep breath and then let it out. "All right, so, what does all of that mean?"

"Harrow and the Crawling Chaos got away," I said. "So the cult will still come after me, but I think... I think that now they've seen I can use some of the power of the curse, they might be more sneaky about it. But the best part is, I'm not nearly as afraid now. I'm not just an ordinary person with no defences against their magic. I can fight back."

"Cedric, this power," Oliver said. "If it's from... uh, the beyond, as you called it. It might be dangerous to use. What if you're somehow, I don't know, increasing the power the curse has? Or increasing the connection this beast thing has with this world? I think you should be very careful about it."

"I agree," Dante said. His tone a little more authoritative. "I could sense when you used the magic, and it didn't taste good."

"You could taste the magic?" Gabriel said, his eyebrow raising.

"In a manner of speaking, yes," Dante said. "I can tell what is witch magic, what is fey magic, what is mer magic... and I can tell what is something dangerous."

"I don't mind being a bit more dangerous," I said. "This last while, you've all been treating me as if I'm fragile, just a thing to be protected. Like I can't be trusted. A child. Gabriel burned my painting!" I hadn't realised that the painting was still a sore spot for me but apparently it was.

"It was a symptom of your curse," Gabriel said. He had the grace to look ashamed though.

"I could have painted over it."

"Cedric, none of us think you're a child," Oliver began.

I swallowed and shook my head. "I just want you all to think of me a bit more as an equal. I know I'm not as handy with a sword, but this is my opportunity, this power, it can help me fight, maybe it's the key to taking down the cult altogether."

Oliver couldn't meet my eye, his jaw was tight.

Gabriel looked troubled. "It's not that I don't think of you as an equal," he said. "I'm sorry if I made you feel that way, Cedric. I want to protect you."

Dante shook his head and sighed. "This power, whatever it is you have in you now, it's like fire. It could consume you. Trust me, I can sense it clearly."

I felt a little diminished by these words. "Well, I wasn't going to go around using it all the time," I said, trying not to whine.

"If you can avoid using it at all, that would be for the best," Dante said. "I'm sorry, I know you feel like it's a gift, but it sounds like just another part of the curse."

"Fine," I said, sticking my hands in my pockets, and feeling the wooden figure, rubbing my index finger over the carved tattoo on its back. I hoped they couldn't tell I was lying. "I won't."

CHAPTER 34

IN WHICH A SIDE OF BEEF IS DEVOURED AND A DRINKING GAME INVENTED

*C*ook took a couple of hours to roast the side of beef and a number of potatoes to go with it. He also made a very fine gravy, and together with the wine barrels and the ale, it was a delicious feast.

The Devil's Whore was anchored and the crew were storytelling, sharing songs and generally celebrating another successful raid of a manor house, and of course, my survival of the ritual. Scratch and Marco were comparing stories of the deep ocean, trying to outdo each other with narrow escapes from monstrous sharks or other predators.

Pilcher seemed to be unable to stop laughing, I wasn't sure exactly what had set him off but he kept getting hold of himself and then bursting into giggles again.

I sat on a bench between Dante and Oliver, who I was relatively sure were giving each other the eye.

My spirits were up, I too, was pleased I had survived the ritual and although we didn't know where the Crawling Chaos and Harrow had gone I had the distinct feeling we'd have something of a reprieve from them. Besides, I was getting rather excited about being the filling in a Dante-and-Oliver sandwich.

Gabriel had been talking with Bilal, but he swaggered over

to us, looking a little less put together and a bit more louche than normal. He had a bottle of ale in his fist.

"I propose a drinking game," he said, his voice not quite at its usual level of control, his smile slightly messy.

"A drinking game?" Oliver repeated.

"Aye, Mister Stanhope." Gabriel extended his hand to Oliver, and to my excitement, he took it. "A game in which we drink."

Dante chuckled and nipped playfully at my shoulder.

"I'm fantastic at drinking games," I said. "I'm always the most drunk."

"I rather think that means you're terrible at them," Dante murmured.

"We're in!"

Gabriel tugged Oliver in closer to him, a certain electricity seemed to pass between them. "And yourself?"

"Absolutely."

"Right, the rules are... wait, we need a challenge... " Gabriel trailed off, frowning for a moment, then he smiled wider. "Right, here's the rules, we cannot use each other's first names, if you do, you drink."

"And you have to take off a piece of clothing," I added. Because the best games I'd played all had that for a forfeit.

Oliver raised his eyebrows. "Maybe we ought to retire to the cabin then?"

Gabriel looked around at the various revelling pirates and shrugged. "If you'd rather not put on a show, I suppose?"

Dante rose and offered me his hand. "Let's go to the cabin, Cedric."

This felt particularly pointed, as I'd just been about to exclaim something along the lines of 'let them look!' But glancing at Oliver told me that he wasn't at all interested in putting on any sort of show, so I took Dante's hand, snagged a large jug of wine in my other and let him guide me towards the Captain's Cabin.

"Hey, you used my first name," I said. "You have to drink and start getting naked now!"

"The game hasn't started yet."

"It started as soon as Gabriel said the rule," I said.

"You just said his first name." Dante tugged me against his chest and kissed me swiftly, barely giving me a chance to register that he'd done it before letting me go. I flushed hot, perhaps for being caught out in the game, or perhaps for being caught out the other way. I swallowed hard.

"Guess we both need to get naked, then."

"One piece of clothing at a time," Oliver followed us into the cabin and Gabriel was last through the door, closing it firmly. The noise of the revel outside got quieter, but I didn't want to let this get awkward. I pressed the jug of wine into Oliver's hands and pulled off the red vest I had on, depositing it on the ground.

Gabriel pulled out a bottle and handed it around. "Spiced rum," he said.

"Your turn…" I remembered just in time not to say Dante's name. "Mister G." I took the rum bottle off Oliver and took a swig, smacking my lips. It was liquid fire, warm and delicious.

"Nice catch, pup." Gabriel took a seat on the bed and leaned back on his hands. Oliver sidled up against me, taking my hand and we watched Dante bend down and with great ceremony remove one of his boots. I hadn't thought to wear shoes on board, which made my being naked first an even greater likelihood.

"Now, Mister Stanhope, there's no need to be concerned," Gabriel said. "It might be your first time in a fourway with pirates, but we'll take good care of you."

Oliver blushed and squeezed my hand a little harder. "I don't mind the number of partners, and I'm not shy," he said, although it was more of a murmur. "It is my first time with Dante though, whoops."

193

He took a swig from my jug as Gabriel laughed. "Clothes off please," I said, giving him a warm smile.

"The vampire is a kitten really," Gabriel said. Dante made an outraged noise of disbelief.

"How dare you say such a thing!" But it wasn't true outrage, there was a twinkle in his eye. The three of us paused in our banter to watch as Oliver removed his glasses and put them on aside.

"That hardly counts!"

"I assure you, it does," Oliver said, primly.

"I am not a kitten," Dante said, suddenly.

"You're a kitten, and it's very endearing," Gabriel said. "Cedric, don't you agree?"

"Ahh you have to drink!" I replied, hurrying over to prod him in the chest. "And let me help you with your shirt." I fumbled with the lacings on his shirt, which were mostly undone as it was. "And for the record," I continued, deliberately not looking at Dante. "You are a little kittenish, when you're being ordered about."

Dante made another indignant noise, and I heard Oliver, his voice a bit more confident. "You like to be ordered about, do you, Dante?"

I kissed Gabriel's chest and then turned to watch Oliver and Dante eying each other. "Oh yes, and Oliver likes to get all bossy," I said. "And rough, almost as much as..." Gabriel's hand closed over my mouth and I felt warmth spread through my nether regions.

"Puppy, the idea of the game is to *not* say people's names, remember?"

It didn't take long at all before we were all more or less naked, and laughing as much as we were drinking. The rum was warming us all up, and Oliver had ordered Dante onto the bed with me and Gabriel. Oliver followed close behind, his hand stroking the cool paleness of Dante's back.

I was down to my drawers and Gabriel's hands were roaming around my hips and arse in a very pleasing way.

In fact Oliver was the only one with a shirt still on, having chosen to keep it on, even while losing trousers and everything else.

He was propped up against the wall, I was situated between Gabriel's legs, and Dante was in the middle of the bed quite naked. I leaned past Dante and rested my head in Oliver's lap. The spiced rum had stolen any hint of cleverness from my tongue, so I simply said...

"Oliver, what's my name? I've forgotten it."

"You're a gigantic goose," Oliver said. But then he smiled indulgently. "And your name is Cedric."

Gabriel whooped and yanked my underthings off for me. I tried to help Oliver with his shirt, but in trying to do so, kneed Dante in the thigh. He caught me around the waist and hauled me in for a kiss. I relaxed into it, winding arms around his neck and moaning.

Gabriel moved closer, the mattress shifting as he caressed my waist and kissed my shoulder.

I turned my head and beckoned to Oliver, who was after all, only inches away but not yet a part of the clinch. "Come and kiss your goose," I said.

He went to his knees and obligingly did so. He tasted the same as Dante, of spiced rum, and it was a flavour I was absolutely loving. I pulled back, gripped Dante by the jaw and aimed him towards Oliver. "Now you two."

They eyed each other, almost shy, which was rather amusing since we were all naked and tangled together.

"Oh go on," Gabriel said, surprising me with his eagerness.

Dante smiled, Oliver tilted his head to the right and they kissed, gently and tentatively, getting to know each other I supposed.

I felt my own heart flutter with excitement, and I realised

just how much I had hoped that all three of these men would get on. And more than that, I *wanted* them to find each other attractive, I wanted them to want each other. It was a strange thing to realise, that although I did desperately want to be the centre of attention, I didn't want only that. I wanted them to … care… yes. I wanted them all to love me, but I wanted them all in love.

Gabriel slipped my collar around my throat and buckled it, and my breath became quite shallow. I turned to him, eyes wide in mock innocence. "What are you doing to me, Captain?"

"Trying to keep you in line." He grinned and kissed me so hard I thought my lips might bruise.

Things became something of a blur after that, the number of hands on me was impossible to keep track of. I was stroking Gabriel's cock for a while, and then sucking on it, while someone stretched me open. Then someone lifted my hips and set me on my knees as I pulled Dante in to kiss my neck, hoping he could find somewhere to bite around the collar.

Someone's mouth found my cock and I looked down to see Oliver, licking me like he was born to it, and I almost orgasmed at the sight of it. Then Gabriel's hand closed around the base of me, holding me back.

Dante's teeth teased at my skin, and I closed my eyes and begged the world in general.

Gabriel moved behind me, pushing Dante aside a little, to push inside me. Oliver pulled back from his work and claimed Dante, the two of them wrapping around each other as Oliver shoved his hips and Dante cried out. I was still on my knees, so I fell forward to kiss first Dante and then Oliver, and then all thought was lost to sensation.

The heat of two bodies, and the coolness of one was almost overwhelming and I found it very hard to catch my breath.

I crashed my wrist against Dante's mouth and he bit down, drinking from me, until Oliver laced his fingers with mine and pulled my arm back, offering his neck to Dante instead. Dante hesitated only a moment before sinking his teeth in, Oliver made a soft noise of ecstasy.

Gabriel's thrusts kept distracting me from the sight of it although I desperately wanted to watch, and I felt myself squeezing and clenching around him. His fingers played and teased at my nipples, and then reached for Oliver's hand, guiding it to my cock.

It seemed as if we all orgasmed together in the same moment, although between all the sensations I couldn't truly say if that was the case. I felt an elbow in my ribs, my knees starting to ache as Gabriel gasped and filled me, and all the moans and bliss melted together into one euphoric noise.

We disentangled partially, negotiating space on the bed. Gabriel extinguished the lantern and I started to drift off, sandwiched happily between my lovers and thanking the universe that this was my life.

"Fantastic drinking game," I managed to mumble before falling asleep.

POST SCRIPT

*T*hat night, something woke me in the early hours of the morning. I was snuggled into Gabriel's side, my head pillowed on his shoulder.

I pushed up to a half sitting position, and looked around. A shape passed the window of the cabin, silhouetted by the lantern light of the dog watch.

A tall, thin man. Painfully tall, taller than Gabriel. The smiling, blue eyed man from St Vincent, he was here, on the Devil's Whore somehow.

The Crawling Chaos.

I know it doesn't sound like much, but your review of this book actually does help. Amazon rewards reviews, and the more a book has, the more sales it gets. Please leave a review or a rating if you can!

The next installment of Cedric's story, Schooled by the Scientist is coming soon, preorder it here:

My Book

Sign up for Drake's newsletter for updates on new releases
https://www.subscribepage.com/q4c4n0
Come join Drake's Crew reader's group to meet other fans and get exclusive content – maybe
you'll even get to name – or become! – a character in the next book
https://www.facebook.com/groups/1272511269588779/

Find Drake online:

Twitter: https://twitter.com/DrakeLamarque
Pinterest: https://www.pinterest.nz/drakelamarque/
Newsletter: https://www.subscribepage.com/q4c4n0
BookBub: https://www.bookbub.com/profile/drake-lamarque
Instagram: https://www.instagram.com/drakelamarque/

ACKNOWLEDGMENTS

This book had a problematic first draft, it was written in a stressful time. I wish to thank Kitty, Liz and Anna for being fantastic readers and giving such valuable feedback. I think it's quite a bit better now.

It's being released in an even more stressful time, and I hope that you can forgive any errors.

GENTLEMAN'S BOUNTY

BOOK 1 - KIDNAPPED BY THE GENTLEMAN

Buy Now

Cedric has been kidnapped by pirates.

...they have no idea how much trouble they're in for.

Cedric was living his best life, partying in the colonies, bedding whomever he pleased and trusting that his parents' money and affluence would get him out of any unfortunate scrapes.

Until he was kidnapped by the fearsome pirate Lucifer, who planned to trade him for a hefty ransom. Unfortunately, he's not the only one after Cedric, and the strange secret society who have Cedric in their sights might just be more dangerous than Captain Lucifer.

Now Cedric is trapped on a pirate ship with a dashingly handsome captain, a quartermaster who won't stop staring at him and an overwhelming desire to find some fun, all while saving his hide from an unknown organisation who will stop at nothing to track him down.

HIS PIRATICAL HAREM

BOOK ONE – CABIN BOY

Buy now

I've never been what I was supposed to be. Wealthy sons of Port Governors aren't supposed to be ejected from the British Navy after less than a year, they're not supposed to like pulp romances or daydream about the handsome heroes of the stories instead of the heroines.

When my Father issued me an order to marry a woman, I knew I had no choice but to make my own way in the world, and I found a berth on the first ship out of Jamaica.

I didn't mean to join a pirate ship, and I certainly didn't intend to find myself the cabin boy to an incredibly charming Pirate Captain. Or that I'd also be attracted to the mysterious First Mate, or that both of them would show me all sorts of unspeakable and salacious pleasures while on board. How can I choose just one of them when I want both?

In addition to confusion on board the ship, there's also enchanting genderfluid merfolk, a cat which seems to understand a lot more than it should, an unseasonable storm and a sea witch with a serious grudge... and with all these complications, I am definitely in over my head.

Come and meet the crew:

Gideon: an innocent with a lot of forbidden desires and a lot of love to give

Tate: a huge, muscular ship's captain with a sweet side

Ezra: a dominant and closed off first mate

Ora: a genderqueer, curious and affectionate merman

HIS PIRATICAL HAREM

BOOK TWO – FIRST MATE'S PET

Buy now

Things were looking good, until the ship's cat became a man...

I didn't mean to join a pirate ship, but now that I'm here, well. Life is pretty good. Between the sexy and intimidating Captain Tate, the mysterious First Mate, Ora the merfolk and now Zeb the ship's cat I'm well entertained.

Rumours abound that the Royal Navy are searching for me at my father's order, and between that, an eventful trip to Tortuga (the famed pirate town) and maintaining the relationships with the crew... I've certainly got my work cut out for me.

∽

Meet the crew:

Gideon: a well bred young man who is discovering his forbidden desires aren't necessarily a problem at sea

Tate: the impressive Captain with a sweet side
Ezra: the controlling and alluring First Mate
Ora: a genderqueer, sweet and mystical merman
Zeb: a cat shifter, who's learning about being human

HIS PIRATICAL HAREM

BOOK THREE - MERFOLK'S MATE

Buy now

The British Navy caught up to the Grey Kelpie, and everything I'd built for my life has fallen apart.

Tate and Ezra are headed for the gallows. Ora has disappeared into an unwelcome sea and I have no idea what's become of the ship's cat...

It's up to me to save them, but I'm trapped on the Naval ship, the same as my lovers. If I'm to get us out of here, I'm going to have to use all my wits, and maybe a little magic?

~

Meet the crew:

Gideon: a well-bred young man discovering a new side of himself

Tate: the sweet Captain with a dark past

Ezra: a dominating First Mate who's slowly finding his soft side

Ora: a mystical merfolk who understands more than the rest

Zeb: an affectionate cat shifter who knows what he wants

Content warning: some knife and blood play in one scene

HIS PIRATICAL HAREM

BOOK FOUR - CAPTAIN'S TREASURE

Buy now

I, Gideon Keene, have two big problems.

Two things, well, people, standing between me and my happiness.

One is a vengeful sea witch called Solomon, who has it in for me and my beloved Captain Tate.

The other is my father.

One has found us, the other is hounding us. It's time to take the battle to them, hold my head high and fight first one, then the other.

But how can a cabin boy, a ship's cat, a member of the merfolk and two pirates defeat the most powerful sea witch in the Caribbean? Tate betrayed him, badly, years ago and now his furious magic has drawn our ship to his blasted islands.

Assuming we survive, then take on the governor of Jamaica, who is determined to see me married to a nice girl and producing heirs?

This is going to take all the courage I have, all the magic I can summon to me, and the wits and understanding of each of my cherished lovers. Not one of us could do it alone, but maybe... just maybe, we can do it together.

Buy now

There are three golden rules for new recruits at Fairyland Theme Park:

1. No breaking character, even if you're dying of heat exhaustion
   2. Always give guests the most magical time
   3. No falling in love.

Nate's only been at work one day, and he's already broken all three.

Fast-tracked into a Prince role, Nate's at odds with Dash, the handsome not-so-charming prince who is supposed to be training him. Nate doesn't know how he ended up on Dash's bad side, but the broody prince sure is hot when he gets mad.

Dash has worked long and hard to play Prince Justice at Fairyland. Now, instead of focusing on his own performance, he is forced to train newbie Nate to be the perfect prince. Nate's annoying ease with the guests coupled with his charm and good looks could dethrone Dash from his number one spot ... so why does he secretly want to kiss him?

Fairyland heats up as sparks fly between the two rival princes. Will they get their fairytale romance before they're kicked out of Fairyland for good?

Find out in this standalone MM contemporary romance by Jaxon Knight, set in an amusement park where fairytales can come true.

ALSO PUBLISHED BY GREY KELPIE STUDIO

MISCHIEF AND MAYHEM BY JAXON KNIGHT

Buy now

Mischief

Protecting royalty at Fairyland theme park seemed about as far from Afghanistan as Cody could get. But the hot new rollercoaster brings up some unexpected trouble - and not the kind of trouble he knows how to handle alone.

Mayhem

Dean loves running the Spaceship Mayhem roller coaster - he gets to meet new people every day! When he sees a handsome, troubled security guard repeatedly fail to ride it, he sees an opportunity to help. And maybe they can be more than friends?

Cody reluctantly accepts cute, boy-next-door Dean's help and sparks fly between them, but between mischief, mayhem and miscommunication, can they ever make a relationship work?

Mischief and Mayhem is a slow burn, opposites attract MM sweet romance featuring snark, foolishness, motorbikes, assumptions, the chicken door and a HEA

RECIPE FOR CHAOS BY JAXON KNIGHT

Buy now

The recipe is simple:
    Charlie cooks an amazing meal
    Charlie impresses heir to the theme park Max Jones
    Charlie gets a promotion and a dash of control over his kitchen

But the perfect recipe becomes unpalatable with one wrong ingredient and Max Jones is not behaving how Charlie expected...

Max is meant to inherit the entire Fairyland theme park but he just wants to party, have fun and bed as many people as possible. That is, until he meets Charlie and falls for him so hard he can't even finish the delicious meal.

Charlie doesn't have time for clubs or helicopter flights over the city, but Max is accustomed to getting what he wants, and he wants Charlie.

Featuring one part Billionaire, one part sensible chef, six cups of attraction, a generous dose of snark and a freshly prepared Happy Ever After.

ALSO PUBLISHED BY GREY KELPIE STUDIO

THE GOOD, THE BAD AND THE DAD BY JAXON KNIGHT

Buy now

Haru is a single dad, a widower, doing his best to balance his career and raising his little girl, Minako. Thankfully Fairyland theme park is a haven for both of them. However, when both a prince and a pirate start courting Haru, his balancing act gets a lot harder...

Cillian plays a pirate at Fairyland theme park and he loves playing the roguish character in and out of work hours. The last thing he wants is to settle down with a guy with a kid, so can't he stop thinking about handsome single dad Haru. And why can't he stop looking at pictures of Prince Magnificence and his stupid symmetrical face? And why does he keep running into both of them?

Grayson feels he's found his home in the role of Prince Magnificence, but he's more likely to run from love than seek it out. Until he meets Haru, that is. Christmas is complicated by Grayson's role being featured in a special Christmas celebration. Not only that, but his feelings for Haru, and his possible rival

Cillian keep on growing. Maybe it's time to stop hiding who he really is?

The Good, the Bad and the Dad is a sweet MMM romance featuring a single father, a rogue and a trans prince with a heart of gold. No cheating, just the tentative first steps into polyamory.